Leaves of Grass

The Original 1855 Edition

DOVER·THRIFT·EDITIONS

Leaves of Grass
The Original 1855 Edition

WALT WHITMAN

DOVER PUBLICATIONS, INC.
Mineola, New York

DOVER THRIFT EDITIONS

GENERAL EDITOR: MARY CAROLYN WALDREP
EDITOR OF THIS VOLUME: JOSLYN T. PINE

Copyright

Copyright © 2007 by Dover Publications, Inc.
All rights reserved.

Bibliographical Note

This Dover edition, first published in 2007, is an unabridged republication of the first edition of the work originally published in 1855 by the author, Brooklyn, New York. The Introductory Note is excerpted from Chapter VIII, "Poe and Whitman," from *The American Spirit in Literature: A Chronicle of Great Interpreters* by Bliss Perry; it was originally published in 1918 by Yale University Press, New Haven, CT.

Library of Congress Cataloging-in-Publication Data

Whitman, Walt, 1819–1892.
    Leaves of grass / Walt Whitman.
        p. cm. — Dover thrift edition
    "The original 1855 edition."
    ISBN-13: 978-0-486-45676-8 (pbk.)
    ISBN-10: 0-486-45676-5 (pbk.)
PS3201 2007
811/.3 22

2006048829

Manufactured in the United States by Courier Corporation
45676504
www.doverpublications.com

INTRODUCTORY NOTE[1]

Walt Whitman

by Bliss Perry

Walt Whitman had a passion for his native soil; he was hypnotized by the word America; he spent much of his mature life in brooding over the question, "What, after all, is an American, and what should an American poet be in our age of science and democracy?" His personality is unique. In many respects he still baffles our curiosity. Whatever our literary students may feel, and whatever foreign critics may assert, it must be acknowledged that to the vast majority of American men and women "good old Walt" is still an outsider.

Let us try to see first the type of mind with which we are dealing. It is fundamentally religious, perceiving the unity and kinship and glory of all created things. It is this passion of worship which inspired St. Francis of Assisi's "Canticle to the Sun." It cries, "Benedicite, Omnia opera Domini: All ye Green Things upon the Earth, bless ye the Lord!" That is the real motto for Whitman's "Leaves of Grass." Like St. Francis, and like his own immediate master, Ralph Waldo Emerson, Whitman is a mystic. He cannot argue the ultimate questions; he asserts them. Instead of marshaling and sifting the proofs for immortality, he chants "I know I am deathless." Like Emerson again, Whitman shares that peculiarly American type of mysticism known as Transcendentalism, but he came at the end of this movement instead of at the beginning of it. In his Romanticism, likewise, he is an end of an era figure. His affiliations with Victor Hugo are significant;

[1] The Introductory Note is excerpted from *The American Spirit in Literature: A Chronicle of Great Interpreters* by Bliss Perry, first published in 1918. The use of ellipsis to denote the few instances of excised text has been dispensed with for the sake of better narrative flow. Perry (1860–1954) was a distinguished scholar and author, especially well-known for his writings on American literature, including a critical biography of Whitman. He taught English at Williams College, and Harvard and Princeton universities, and was the eighth editor of the *Atlantic Monthly* (1899–1909). [ED.]

and a volume of Scott's poems which he owned at the age of sixteen became his "inexhaustible mine and treasury for more than sixty years." Finally, and quite as uncompromisingly as Emerson, Thoreau, and Poe, Whitman is an individualist. He represents the assertive, Jacksonian period of our national existence. In a thousand similes he makes a declaration of independence for the separate person, the "single man" of Emerson's Phi Beta Kappa address. "I wear my hat as I please, indoors and out." Sometimes this is mere swagger. Sometimes it is superb.

So much for the type. Let us turn next to the story of Whitman's life. It must here be told in the briefest fashion, for Whitman's own prose and poetry relate the essentials of his biography. He was born on Long Island, of New England and Dutch ancestry, in 1819. Whitman's father was a carpenter, who "leaned to the Quakers." There were many children. When little "Walt"—as he was called, to distinguish him from his father, Walter—was four, the family moved to Brooklyn. The boy had scanty schooling, and by the time he was twenty had tried typesetting, teaching, and editing a country newspaper on Long Island. He was a big, dark-haired fellow, sensitive, emotional, extraordinarily impressible.

The next sixteen years were full of happy vagrancy. At twenty-two he was editing a paper in New York, and furnishing short stories to the "Democratic Review," a literary journal which numbered Bryant, Longfellow, Whittier, Poe, Hawthorne, and Thoreau among its contributors. He wrote a novel on temperance, "mostly in the reading-room of Tammany Hall," and tried here and there an experiment in free verse. He was in love with the pavements of New York and the Brooklyn ferryboats, in love with Italian opera and with long tramps over Long Island. He left his position on "The Brooklyn Eagle" and wandered south to New Orleans. By and by he drifted back to New York, tried lecturing, worked at the carpenter's trade with his father, and brooded over a book—"a book of new things."

This was the famous "Leaves of Grass." He set the type himself, in a Brooklyn printing-office, and printed about eight hundred copies. The book had a portrait of the author—a meditative, gray-bearded poet in workman's clothes—and a confused preface on America as a field for the true poet. Then followed the new gospel, "I celebrate myself," chanted in long lines of free verse, whose patterns perplexed contemporary readers. For the most part it was passionate speech rather than song, a rhapsodical declamation in hybrid rhythms. Very few people bought the book or pretended to understand what it was all about. Some were startled by the frank sexuality of certain poems. But Emerson wrote to Whitman from Concord: "I find it the most extraordinary piece of wit and wisdom that America has yet contributed."

Until the Civil War was half over, Whitman remained in Brooklyn, patiently composing new poems for successive printings of his book. Then he went to the front to care for a wounded brother, and finally settled down in a Washington garret to spend his strength as an army hospital nurse. He wrote "Drum Taps" and other magnificent poems about the War, culminating in his threnody on Lincoln's death, "When Lilacs last in the Dooryard Bloomed." Swinburne called this "the most sonorous nocturn ever chanted in the church of the world." After the war had ended, Whitman stayed on in Washington as a government clerk, and saw much of John Burroughs[2] and W. D. O'Connor.[3] John Hay[4] was a staunch friend. Some of the best known poets and critics of England and the Continent now began to recognize his genius. But his health had been permanently shattered by his heroic service as a nurse, and in 1873 he suffered a paralytic stroke which forced him to resign his position in Washington and remove to his brother's home in Camden, New Jersey.

He was only fifty-four, but his best work was already done, and his remaining years, until his death in 1892, were those of patient and serene invalidism. He wrote some fascinating prose in this final period, and his cluttered chamber in Camden became the shrine of many a literary pilgrim, among them some of the foremost men of letters of this country and of Europe. He was cared for by loyal friends. Occasionally he appeared in public, a magnificent gray figure of a man. And then, at seventy-three, the "Dark mother always gliding near" enfolded him.

There are puzzling things in the physical and moral constitution of Walt Whitman, and the obstinate questions involved in his theory of poetry and in his actual poetical performance are still far from solution. But a few points concerning him are by this time fairly clear. They must be swiftly summarized.

---

[2]John Burroughs (1837–1921) was a famed naturalist, poet and writer, who was a close friend and great admirer of Whitman. He produced the first biographical study of the artist, *Notes on Walt Whitman, As Poet and Person* (1867). [ED.]

[3]Willam Douglas O'Connor (1832–1889) was a newspaperman, writer and government clerk who helped Whitman obtain a job at the Indian Affairs Bureau of the Department of the Interior. He later defended him in print (*The Good Gray Poet: A Vindication*, 1866) when Whitman was dismissed because the *Leaves of Grass* was generally deemed "obscene," and put his own career at risk when he found him another job in the Attorney General's office. [ED.]

[4]John [Milton] Hay (1838–1905) was a lawyer, writer, diplomat and U.S. Secretary of State (1898–1905) who helped implement the Open Door policy under Theodore Roosevelt. [ED.]

The first obstacle to the popular acceptance of Walt Whitman is the formlessness or alleged formlessness of "Leaves of Grass." This is a highly technical question, involving a more accurate notation than has thus far been made of the patterns and tunes of free verse and of emotional prose. Whitman's "new and national declamatory expression," as he termed it, cannot receive a final technical valuation until we have made more scientific progress in the analysis of rhythms. As regards the contents of his verse, it is plain that he included much material unfused and untransformed by emotion. These elements foreign to the nature of poetry clog many of his lines. The enumerated objects in his catalogue or inventory poems often remain inert objects only. Like many mystics, he was hypnotized by external phenomena, and he often fails to communicate to his reader the trancelike emotion which he himself experienced. This imperfect transfusion of his material is a far more significant defect in Whitman's poetry than the relatively few passages of unashamed sexuality which shocked the American public in 1855.

The gospel or burden of "Leaves of Grass" is no more difficult of comprehension than the general drift of Emerson's essays, which helped to inspire it. The starting point of the book is a mystical illumination regarding the unity and blessedness of the universe, an insight passing understanding, but based upon the revelatory experience of love. In the light of this experience, all created things are recognized as divine. The starting-point and center of the Whitman world is the individual man, the "strong person," imperturbable in mind, athletic in body, unconquerable, and immortal. Such individuals meet in comradeship, and pass together along the open roads of the world. No one is excluded because of his poverty or his sins; there is room in the ideal America for everybody except the doubter and sceptic. Whitman does not linger over the smaller groups of human society, like the family. He is not a fireside poet. He passes directly from his strong persons, meeting freely on the open road, to his conception of "these States." One of his typical visions of the breadth and depth and height of America will be found in "By Blue Ontario's Shore." In this and in many similar rhapsodies Whitman holds obstinately to what may be termed the three points of his national creed. The first is the newness of America, and its expression is in his well-known chant of "Pioneers, O Pioneers." Yet this new America is subtly related to the past; and in Whitman's later poems, such as "Passage to India," the spiritual kinship of orient and occident is emphasized. The second article of the creed is the unity of America. Here he voices the conceptions of Hamilton, Clay, Webster, and Lincoln. In spite of all diversity in external aspects the republic is "one and indivisible." This unity, in Whitman's view, was cemented forever by the issue of the Civil War. Lincoln, the "Captain," dies indeed on the deck of the "victor ship," but the ship comes into the harbor "with object won." Third and finally, Whitman insists upon the solidarity of America with all countries of the globe. Particularly in his yearning and thoughtful old age, the poet perceived that humanity has but one heart and that it should have but one will. No American poet has ever prophesied so directly and powerfully concerning the final issue involved in that World War which he did not live to see.

Whitman had defects of character and defects of art. His life and work raise many problems which will long continue to fascinate and to baffle the critics. But after all of them have had their say, it will remain true that he was a seer and a prophet, far in advance of his own time, like Lincoln, and like Lincoln, an inspired interpreter of the soul of this republic.

Leaves of Grass
The Original 1855 Edition

Aforms or amid other politics or the idea of castes or the old religions . . . accepts the lesson with calmness . . . is not so impatient as has been supposed that the slough still sticks to opinions and manners and literature while the life which served its requirements has passed into the new life of the new forms . . . perceives that the corpse is slowly borne from the eating and sleeping rooms of the house . . . perceives that it waits a little while in the door . . . that it was fittest for its days . . . that its action has descended to the stalwart and wellshaped heir who approaches . . . and that he shall be fittest for his days.

The Americans of all nations at any time upon the earth have probably the fullest poetical nature. The United States themselves are essentially the greatest poem. In the history of the earth hitherto the largest and most stirring appear tame and orderly to their ampler largeness and stir. Here at last is something in the doings of man that corresponds with the broadcast doings of the day and night. Here is not merely a nation but a teeming nation of nations. Here is action untied from strings necessarily blind to particulars and details magnificently moving in vast masses. Here is the hospitality which forever indicates heroes. . . . Here are the roughs and beards and space and ruggedness and nonchalance that the soul loves. Here the performance disdaining the trivial unapproached in the tremendous audacity of its crowds and groupings and the push of its perspective spreads with crampless and flowing breadth and showers its prolific and splendid extravagance. One sees it must indeed own the riches of the summer and winter, and need never be bankrupt while corn grows from the ground or the orchards drop apples or the bays contain fish or men beget children upon women.

Other states indicate themselves in their deputies . . . but the genius of the United States is not best or most in its executives or legislatures, nor in its ambassadors or authors or colleges or churches or parlors, nor even in its newspapers or inventors . . . but always most in the common people. Their manners speech dress friendships—the freshness and candor of their physiognomy—the picturesque looseness of their carriage . . . their deathless attachment to freedom—their aversion to anything indecorous or soft or mean—the practical acknowledgment of the citizens of one state by the citizens of all other states—the fierceness of their roused resentment—their curiosity and welcome of novelty—their self-esteem and wonderful sympathy—their susceptibility to a slight—the air they have of persons who never knew how it felt to stand in the presence of superiors—the fluency of their speech—their delight in music, the sure symptom of manly tenderness and native elegance of soul . . . their good temper and openhandedness—the terrible significance of their elections—the President's taking off his hat to them not they to him—these too are unrhymed poetry. It awaits the gigantic and generous treatment worthy of it.

The largeness of nature or the nation were monstrous without a corresponding largeness and generosity of the spirit of the citizen. Not nature nor swarming states nor streets and steamships nor prosperous business nor farms nor capital nor learning may suffice for the ideal of man . . . nor suffice the poet. No reminiscences may suffice either. A live nation can always cut a deep mark and can have the best authority the cheapest . . . namely from its own soul. This is the sum of the profitable uses of individuals or states and of present action and grandeur and of the subjects of poets.—As if it were necessary to trot back generation after generation to the eastern records! As if the beauty and sacredness of the demonstrable must fall behind that of the mythical! As if men do not make their mark out of any times! As if the opening of the western continent by discovery and what has transpired since in North and South America were less than the small theatre of the antique or the aimless sleepwalking of the middle ages! The pride of the United States leaves the wealth and finesse of the cities and all returns of commerce and agriculture and all the magnitude of geography or shows of exterior victory to enjoy the breed of fullsized men or one fullsized man unconquerable and simple.

The American poets are to enclose old and new for America is the race of races. Of them a bard is to be commensurate with a people. To him the other continents arrive as contributions . . . he gives them reception for their sake and his own sake. His spirit responds to his country's spirit . . . he incarnates its geography and natural life and rivers and lakes. Mississippi with annual freshets and changing chutes, Missouri and Columbia and Ohio and Saint Lawrence with the falls and beautiful masculine Hudson, do not embouchure where they spend themselves more than they embouchure into him. The blue breadth over the inland sea of Virginia and Maryland and the sea off Massachusetts and Maine and over Manhattan bay and over

Champlain and Erie and over Ontario and Huron and Michigan and Superior, and over the Texan and Mexican and Floridian and Cuban seas and over the seas off California and Oregon, is not tallied by the blue breadth of the waters below more than the breadth of above and below is tallied by him. When the long Atlantic coast stretches longer and the Pacific coast stretches longer he easily stretches with them north or south. He spans between them also from east to west and reflects what is between them. On him rise solid growths that offset the growths of pine and cedar and hemlock and liveoak and locust and chestnut and cypress and hickory and limetree and cottonwood and tuliptree and cactus and wildvine and tamarind and persimmon . . . and tangles as tangled as any canebrake or swamp . . . and forests coated with transparent ice and icicles hanging from the boughs and crackling in the wind . . . and sides and peaks of mountains . . . and pasturage sweet and free as savannah or upland or prairie . . . with flights and songs and screams that answer those of the wildpigeon and highhold and orchard oriole and coot and surf-duck and redshouldered-hawk and fish-hawk and white-ibis and indian-hen and cat-owl and water-pheasant and qua-bird and pied-sheldrake and blackbird and mockingbird and buzzard and condor and night-heron and eagle. To him the hereditary countenance descends both mother's and father's. To him enter the essences of the real things and past and present events—of the enormous diversity of temperature and agriculture and mines—the tribes of red aborigines—the weatherbeaten vessels entering new ports or making landings on rocky coasts—the first settlements north or south—the rapid stature and muscle—the haughty defiance of '76, and the war and peace and formation of the constitution . . . the union always surrounded by blatherers and always calm and impregnable—the perpetual coming of immigrants—the wharfhem'd cities and superior marine—the unsurveyed interior—the loghouses and clearings and wild animals and hunters and trappers . . . the free commerce—the fisheries and whaling and gold-digging—the endless gestation of new states—the convening of Congress every December, the members duly coming up from all climates and the uttermost parts . . . the noble character of the young mechanics and of all free American workmen and workwomen . . . the general ardor and friendliness and enterprise—the perfect equality of the female with the male . . . the large amativeness—the fluid movement of the population—the factories and mercantile life and laborsaving machinery—the Yankee swap—the New-York firemen and the target excursion—the southern plantation life—the character of the northeast and of the northwest and southwest—slavery and the tremulous spreading of hands to protect it, and the stern opposition to it which shall never cease till it ceases or the speaking of tongues and the moving of lips cease. For such the expression of the American poet is to be transcendant and new. It is to be indirect and not direct or descriptive or epic. Its quality goes through these to much more. Let the age and wars of other nations be chanted and their eras and characters be illustrated and that finish the verse. Not so the great psalm of the republic. Here the theme is creative and has vista. Here comes one among the wellbeloved stonecutters and plans with decision and science and sees the solid and beautiful forms of the future where there are now no solid forms.

Of all nations the United States with veins full of poetical stuff most need poets and will doubtless have the greatest and use them the greatest. Their Presidents shall not be their common referee so much as their poets shall. Of all mankind the great poet is the equable man. Not in him but off from him things are grotesque or eccentric or fail of their sanity. Nothing out of its place is good and nothing in its place is bad. He bestows on every object or quality its fit proportions neither more nor less. He is the arbiter of the diverse and he is the key. He is the equalizer of his age and land ... he supplies what wants supplying and checks what wants checking. If peace is the routine out of him speaks the spirit of peace, large, rich, thrifty, building vast and populous cities, encouraging agriculture and the arts and commerce— lighting the study of man, the soul, immortality—federal, state or municipal government, marriage, health, freetrade, intertravel by land and sea ... nothing too close, nothing too far off ... the stars not too far off. In war he is the most deadly force of the war. Who recruits him recruits horse and foot ... he fetches parks of artillery the best that engineer ever knew. If the time becomes slothful and heavy he knows how to arouse it ... he can make every word he speaks draw blood. Whatever stagnates in the flat of custom or obedience or legislation he never stagnates. Obedience does not master him, he masters it. High up out of reach he stands turning a concentrated light ... he turns the pivot with his finger ... he baffles the swiftest runners as he stands and easily overtakes and envelops them. The time straying toward infidelity and confections and persiflage he withholds by his steady faith ... he spreads out his dishes ... he offers the sweet firm-fibred meat that grows men and women. His brain is the ultimate brain. He is no arguer ... he is judgment. He judges not as the judge judges but as the sun falling around a helpless thing. As he sees the farthest he has the most faith. His thoughts are the hymns of the praise of things. In the talk on the soul and eternity and God off of his equal plane he is silent. He sees eternity less like a play with a prologue and denouement ... he sees eternity in men and women ... he does not see men and women as dreams or dots. Faith is the antiseptic of the soul ... it pervades the common people and preserves them ... they never give up believing and expecting and trusting. There is that indescribable freshness and unconsciousness about an illiterate person that humbles and mocks the power of the noblest expressive genius. The poet sees for a certainty how one not a great artist may be just as sacred and perfect as the greatest artist. ... The power to destroy or remould is freely used by him but never the power of attack. What is past is past. If he does not expose superior models and prove himself by every step he takes he is not what is wanted. The presence of the greatest poet conquers ... not parleying or struggling or any prepared attempts. Now he has passed that way see after him! there is not left any vestige of despair or misanthropy or cunning or exclusiveness or the ignominy of a nativity or color or delusion of hell or the necessity of hell ... and no man thenceforward shall be degraded for ignorance or weakness or sin.

The greatest poet hardly knows pettiness or triviality. If he breathes into any thing that was before thought small it dilates with the grandeur and life of the universe. He is a seer ... he is individual ... he is complete in himself ... the others are as good as he, only he sees it and they do not. He is not one of the chorus ... he does not stop for any regulation ... he is the president of regulation. What the eyesight does to the rest he does to the rest. Who knows the curious mystery of the eyesight? The other senses corroborate themselves, but this is removed from any proof but its own and foreruns the identities of the spiritual world. A single glance of it mocks all the investigations of man and all the instruments and books of the earth and all reasoning. What is marvellous? what is unlikely? what is impossible or baseless or vague? after you have once just opened the space of a peach-pit and given audience to far and near and to the sunset and had all things enter with electric swiftness softly and duly without confusion or jostling or jam.

The land and sea, the animals fishes and birds, the sky of heaven and the orbs, the forests mountains and rivers, are not small themes ... but folks expect of the poet to indicate more than the beauty and dignity which always attach to dumb real objects ... they expect him to indicate the path between reality and their souls. Men and women perceive the beauty well enough ... probably as well as he. The passionate tenacity of hunters, woodmen, early risers, cultivators of gardens and orchards and fields, the love of healthy women for the manly form, seafaring persons, drivers of horses, the passion for light and the open air, all is an old varied sign of the unfailing perception of beauty and of a residence of the poetic in outdoor people. They can never be assisted by poets to perceive . . . some may but they never can. The poetic quality is not marshalled in rhyme or uniformity or abstract addresses to things nor in melancholy complaints or good precepts, but is the life of these and much else and is in the soul. The profit of rhyme is that it drops seeds of a sweeter and more luxuriant rhyme, and of uniformity that it conveys itself into its own roots in the ground out of sight. The rhyme and uniformity of perfect poems show the free growth of metrical laws and bud from them as unerringly and loosely as lilacs or roses on a bush, and take shapes as compact as the shapes of chestnuts and oranges and melons and pears, and shed the perfume impalpable to form. The fluency and ornaments of the finest poems or music or orations or recitations are not independent but dependent. All beauty comes from beautiful blood and a beautiful brain. If the greatnesses are in conjunction in a man or woman it is enough . . . the fact will prevail through the universe . . . but the gaggery and gilt of a million years will not prevail. Who troubles himself about his ornaments or fluency is lost. This is what you shall do: Love the earth and sun and the animals, despise riches, give alms to every one that asks, stand up for the stupid and crazy, devote your income and labor to others, hate tyrants, argue not concerning God, have patience and indulgence toward the people, take off your hat to nothing known or unknown or to any man or number of men, go freely with powerful uneducated persons and with the young and with the mothers of families, read these leaves in the open air every season of every year of your life, re-examine all you have been told at school or church or in any book, dismiss whatever insults your own soul, and your very flesh shall be a great poem and have the richest fluency not only in its words but in the silent lines of its lips and face and between the lashes of your eyes and in every motion and joint of your body. . . . The poet shall not spend his time in unneeded work. He shall know that the ground is always ready ploughed and manured . . . others may not know it but he shall. He shall go directly to the creation. His trust shall master the trust of everything he touches . . . and shall master all attachment.

The known universe has one complete lover and that is the greatest poet. He consumes an eternal passion and is indifferent which chance happens and which possible contingency of fortune or misfortune and persuades daily and hourly his delicious pay. What balks or breaks others is fuel for his burning progress to contact and amorous joy. Other proportions of the reception of pleasure dwindle to nothing to his proportions. All expected from heaven or from the highest he is rapport with in the sight of the daybreak or a scene of the winter woods or the presence of children playing or with his arm round the neck of a man or woman. His love above all love has leisure and expanse . . . he leaves room ahead of himself. He is no irresolute or suspicious lover . . . he is sure . . . he scorns intervals. His experience and the showers and thrills are not for nothing. Nothing can jar him . . . suffering and darkness cannot—death and fear cannot. To him complaint and jealousy and envy are corpses buried and rotten in the earth . . . he saw them buried. The sea is not surer of the shore or the shore of the sea than he is of the fruition of his love and of all perfection and beauty.

The fruition of beauty is no chance of hit or miss . . . it is inevitable as life . . . it is exact and plumb as gravitation. From the eyesight proceeds another eyesight and from the hearing proceeds another hearing and from the voice proceeds another voice eternally curious of the harmony of things with man. To these respond perfections not only in the committees that were supposed to stand for the rest but in the rest themselves just the same. These understand the law of perfection in masses and floods . . . that its finish is to each for itself and onward from itself . . . that it is profuse and impartial . . . that there is not a minute of the light or dark nor an acre of the earth or sea without it—nor any direction of the sky nor any trade or employment nor any turn of events. This is the reason that about the proper expression of beauty there is precision and balance . . . one part does not need to be thrust above another. The best singer is not the one who has the most lithe and powerful organ . . . the pleasure of poems is not in them that take the handsomest measure and similes and sound.

Without effort and without exposing in the least how it is done the greatest poet brings the spirit of any or all events and passions and scenes and persons some more and some less to bear on your individual character as you hear or read. To do this well is to compete with the laws that pursue and follow time. What is the purpose must surely be there and the clue of it must be there . . . and the faintest indication is the indication of the best and then becomes the clearest indication. Past and present and future are not disjoined but joined. The greatest poet forms the consistence of what is to be from what has been and is. He drags the dead out of their coffins and stands them again on their feet . . . he says to the past, Rise and walk before me that I may realize you. He learns the lesson . . . he places himself where the future becomes present. The greatest poet does not only dazzle his rays over character and scenes and passions . . . he finally ascends and finishes all . . . he exhibits the pinnacles that no man can tell what they are for or what is beyond . . . he glows a moment on the extremest verge. He is most wonderful in his last half-hidden smile or frown . . . by that flash of the moment of parting the one that sees it shall be en-

couraged or terrified afterward for many years. The greatest poet does
not moralize or make applications of morals . . . he knows the soul.
The soul has that measureless pride which consists in never acknowl-
edging any lessons but its own. But it has sympathy as measureless as
its pride and the one balances the other and neither can stretch too
far while it stretches in company with the other. The inmost secrets
of art sleep with the twain. The greatest poet has lain close betwixt
both and they are vital in his style and thoughts.

The art of art, the glory of expression and the sunshine of the light
of letters is simplicity. Nothing is better than simplicity . . . nothing
can make up for excess or for the lack of definiteness. To carry on the
heave of impulse and pierce intellectual depths and give all subjects
their articulations are powers neither common nor very uncommon.
But to speak in literature with the perfect rectitude and insousiance of
the movements of animals and the unimpeachableness of the senti-
ment of trees in the woods and grass by the roadside is the flawless tri-
umph of art. If you have looked on him who has achieved it you have
looked on one of the masters of the artists of all nations and times.
You shall not contemplate the flight of the graygull over the bay or
the mettlesome action of the blood horse or the tall leaning of sun-
flowers on their stalk or the appearance of the sun journeying through
heaven or the appearance of the moon afterward with any more sat-
isfaction than you shall contemplate him. The greatest poet has less a
marked style and is more the channel of thoughts and things without
increase or diminution, and is the free channel of himself. He swears
to his art, I will not be meddlesome, I will not have in my writing any
elegance or effect or originality to hang in the way between me and
the rest like curtains. I will have nothing hang in the way, not the rich-
est curtains. What I tell I tell for precisely what it is. Let who may
exalt or startle or fascinate or sooth I will have purposes as health or
heat or snow has and be as regardless of observation. What I experi-
ence or portray shall go from my composition without a shred of my
composition. You shall stand by my side and look in the mirror with
me.

The old red blood and stainless gentility of great poets will be
proved by their unconstraint. A heroic person walks at his ease
through and out of that custom or precedent or authority that suits
him not. Of the traits of the brotherhood of writers savans musicians
inventors and artists nothing is finer than silent defiance advancing
from new free forms. In the need of poems philosophy politics mech-
anism science behaviour, the craft of art, an appropriate native grand-
opera, shipcraft, or any craft, he is greatest forever and forever who
contributes the greatest original practical example. The cleanest ex-

pression is that which finds no sphere worthy of itself and makes one.

The messages of great poets to each man and woman are, Come to us on equal terms, Only then can you understand us, We are no better than you, What we enclose you enclose, What we enjoy you may enjoy. Did you suppose there could be only one Supreme? We affirm there can be unnumbered Supremes, and that one does not countervail another any more than one eyesight countervails another . . . and that men can be good or grand only of the consciousness of their supremacy within them. What do you think is the grandeur of storms and dismemberments and the deadliest battles and wrecks and the wildest fury of the elements and the power of the sea and the motion of nature and of the throes of human desires and dignity and hate and love? It is that something in the soul which says, Rage on, Whirl on, I tread master here and everywhere, Master of the spasms of the sky and of the shatter of the sea, Master of nature and passion and death, And of all terror and all pain.

The American bards shall be marked for generosity and affection and for encouraging competitors . . . They shall be kosmos . . . without monopoly or secresy . . . glad to pass any thing to any one . . . hungry for equals night and day. They shall not be careful of riches and privilege . . . they shall be riches and privilege . . . they shall perceive who the most affluent man is. The most affluent man is he that confronts all the shows he sees by equivalents out of the stronger wealth of himself. The American bard shall delineate no class of persons nor one or two out of the strata of interests nor love most nor truth most nor the soul most nor the body most . . . and not be for the eastern states more than the western or the northern states more than the southern.

Exact science and its practical movements are no checks on the greatest poet but always his encouragement and support. The outset and remembrance are there . . . there the arms that lifted him first and brace him best . . . there he returns after all his goings and comings. The sailor and traveler . . . the anatomist chemist astronomer geologist phrenologist spiritualist mathematician historian and lexicographer are not poets, but they are the lawgivers of poets and their construction underlies the structure of every perfect poem. No matter what rises or is uttered they sent the seed of the conception of it . . . of them and by them stand the visible proofs of souls . . . always of their fatherstuff must be begotten the sinewy races of bards. If there shall be love and content between the father and the son and if the greatness of the son is the exuding of the greatness of the father there shall be love between the poet and the man of demonstrable science. In the beauty of poems are the tuft and final applause of science.

Great is the faith of the flush of knowledge and of the investigation of the depths of qualities and things. Cleaving and circling here swells the soul of the poet yet is president of itself always. The depths are fathomless and therefore calm. The innocence and nakedness are resumed . . . they are neither modest nor immodest. The whole theory of the special and supernatural and all that was twined with it or educed out of it departs as a dream. What has ever happened . . . what happens and whatever may or shall happen, the vital laws enclose all . . . they are sufficient for any case and for all cases . . . none to be hurried or retarded . . . any miracle of affairs or persons inadmissible in the vast clear scheme where every motion and every spear of grass and the frames and spirits of men and women and all that concerns them are unspeakably perfect miracles all referring to all and each distinct and in its place. It is also not consistent with the reality of the soul to admit that there is anything in the known universe more divine than men and women.

Men and women and the earth and all upon it are simply to be taken as they are, and the investigation of their past and present and future shall be unintermitted and shall be done with perfect candor. Upon this basis philosophy speculates ever looking toward the poet, ever regarding the eternal tendencies of all toward happiness never inconsistent with what is clear to the senses and to the soul. For the eternal tendencies of all toward happiness make the only point of sane philosophy. Whatever comprehends less than that . . . whatever is less than the laws of light and of astronomical motion . . . or less than the laws that follow the thief the liar the glutton and the drunkard through this life and doubtless afterward . . . or less than vast stretches of time or the slow formation of density or the patient upheaving of strata—is of no account. Whatever would put God in a poem or system of philosophy as contending against some being or influence is also of no account. Sanity and ensemble characterise the great master . . . spoilt in one principle all is spoilt. The great master has nothing to do with miracles. He sees health for himself in being one of the mass . . . he sees the hiatus in singular eminence. To the perfect shape comes common ground. To be under the general law is great for that is to correspond with it. The master knows that he is unspeakably great and that all are unspeakably great . . . that nothing for instance is greater than to conceive children and bring them up well . . . that to be is just as great as to perceive or tell.

In the make of the great masters the idea of political liberty is indispensible. Liberty takes the adherence of heroes wherever men and women exist . . . but never takes any adherence or welcome from the rest more than from poets. They are the voice and exposition of lib-

erty. They out of ages are worthy the grand idea . . . to them it is con-
fided and they must sustain it. Nothing has precedence of it and noth-
ing can warp or degrade it. The attitude of great poets is to cheer up
slaves and horrify despots. The turn of their necks, the sound of their
feet, the motions of their wrists, are full of hazard to the one and hope
to the other. Come nigh them awhile and though they neither speak
or advise you shall learn the faithful American lesson. Liberty is
poorly served by men whose good intent is quelled from one failure
or two failures or any number of failures, or from the casual indiffer-
ence or ingratitude of the people, or from the sharp show of the
tushes of power, or the bringing to bear soldiers and cannon or any
penal statutes. Liberty relies upon itself, invites no one, promises noth-
ing, sits in calmness and light, is positive and composed, and knows no
discouragement. The battle rages with many a loud alarm and fre-
quent advance and retreat . . . the enemy triumphs . . . the prison, the
handcuffs, the iron necklace and anklet, the scaffold, garrote and lead-
balls do their work . . . the cause is asleep . . . the strong throats are
choked with their own blood . . . the young men drop their eyelashes
toward the ground when they pass each other . . . and is liberty gone
out of that place? No never. When liberty goes it is not the first to go
nor the second or third to go . . . it waits for all the rest to go . . . it is
the last. . . . When the memories of the old martyrs are faded utterly
away . . . when the large names of patriots are laughed at in the pub-
lic halls from the lips of the orators . . . when the boys are no more
christened after the same but christened after tyrants and traitors in-
stead . . . when the laws of the free are grudgingly permitted and laws
for informers and bloodmoney are sweet to the taste of the people . . .
when I and you walk abroad upon the earth stung with compassion
at the sight of numberless brothers answering our equal friendship and
calling no man master—and when we are elated with noble joy at the
sight of slaves . . . when the soul retires in the cool communion of the
night and surveys its experience and has much extasy over the word
and deed that put back a helpless innocent person into the gripe of
the gripers or into any cruel inferiority . . . when those in all parts of
these states who could easier realize the true American character but
do not yet—when the swarms of cringers, suckers, doughfaces, lice of
politics, planners of sly involutions for their own preferment to city
offices or state legislatures or the judiciary or congress or the presi-
dency, obtain a response of love and natural deference from the peo-
ple whether they get the offices or no . . . when it is better to be a
bound booby and rogue in office at a high salary than the poorest free
mechanic or farmer with his hat unmoved from his head and firm eyes
and a candid and generous heart . . . and when servility by town or

state or the federal government or any oppression on a large scale or small scale can be tried on without its own punishment following duly after in exact proportion against the smallest chance of escape . . . or rather when all life and all the souls of men and women are discharged from any part of the earth—then only shall the instinct of liberty be discharged from that part of the earth.

As the attributes of the poets of the kosmos concentre in the real body and soul and in the pleasure of things they possess the superiority of genuineness over all fiction and romance. As they emit themselves facts are showered over with light . . . the daylight is lit with more volatile light . . . also the deep between the setting and rising sun goes deeper many fold. Each precise object or condition or combination or process exhibits a beauty . . . the multiplication table its—old age its—the carpenter's trade its—the grand-opera its . . . the huge-hulled cleanshaped New-York clipper at sea under steam or full sail gleams with unmatched beauty . . . the American circles and large harmonies of government gleam with theirs . . . and the commonest definite intentions and actions with theirs. The poets of the kosmos advance through all interpositions and coverings and turmoils and stratagems to first principles. They are of use . . . they dissolve poverty from its need and riches from its conceit. You large proprietor they say shall not realize or perceive more than any one else. The owner of the library is not he who holds a legal title to it having bought and paid for it. Any one and every one is owner of the library who can read the same through all the varieties of tongues and subjects and styles, and in whom they enter with ease and take residence and force toward paternity and maternity, and make supple and powerful and rich and large. . . . These American states strong and healthy and accomplished shall receive no pleasure from violations of natural models and must not permit them. In paintings or mouldings or carvings in mineral or wood, or in the illustrations of books or newspapers, or in any comic or tragic prints, or in the patterns of woven stuffs or any thing to beautify rooms or furniture or costumes, or to put upon cornices or monuments or on the prows or sterns of ships, or to put anywhere before the human eye indoors or out, that which distorts honest shapes or which creates unearthly beings or places or contingencies is a nuisance and revolt. Of the human form especially it is so great it must never be made ridiculous. Of ornaments to a work nothing outre can be allowed . . . but those ornaments can be allowed that conform to the perfect facts of the open air and that flow out of the nature of the work and come irrepressibly from it and are necessary to the completion of the work. Most works are most beautiful without ornament. . . . Exaggerations will be revenged in human physiology. Clean and vigorous children are jetted and conceived only in those communities where the models of natural forms are public every day. . . . Great genius and the people of these states must never be demeaned to romances. As soon as histories are properly told there is no more need of romances.

The great poets are also to be known by the absence in them of tricks and by the justification of perfect personal candor. Then folks echo a new cheap joy and a divine voice leaping from their brains: How beautiful is candor! All faults may be forgiven of him who has perfect candor. Henceforth let no man of us lie, for we have seen that openness wins the inner and outer world and that there is no single exception, and that never since our earth gathered itself in a mass have deceit or subterfuge or prevarication attracted its smallest particle or the faintest tinge of a shade—and that through the enveloping wealth and rank of a state or the whole republic of states a sneak or sly person shall be discovered and despised . . . and that the soul has never been once fooled and never can be fooled . . . and thrift without the loving nod of the soul is only a fœtid puff . . . and there never grew up in any of the continents of the globe nor upon any planet or satellite or star, nor upon the asteroids, nor in any part of ethereal space, nor in the midst of density, nor under the fluid wet of the sea, nor in that condition which precedes the birth of babes, nor at any time during the changes of life, nor in that condition that follows what we term death, nor in any stretch of abeyance or action afterward of vitality, nor in any process of formation or reformation anywhere, a being whose instinct hated the truth.

Extreme caution or prudence, the soundest organic health, large hope and comparison and fondness for women and children, large alimentiveness and destructiveness and causality, with a perfect sense of the oneness of nature and the propriety of the same spirit applied to human affairs . . . these are called up of the float of the brain of the world to be parts of the greatest poet from his birth out of his mother's womb and from her birth out of her mother's. Caution seldom goes far enough. It has been thought that the prudent citizen was the citizen who applied himself to solid gains and did well for himself and his family and completed a lawful life without debt or crime. The greatest poet sees and admits these economies as he sees the economies of food and sleep, but has higher notions of prudence than to think he gives much when he gives a few slight attentions at the latch of the gate. The premises of the prudence of life are not the hospitality of it or the ripeness and harvest of it. Beyond the independence of a little sum laid aside for burial-money, and of a few clapboards around and shingles overhead on a lot of American soil owned, and the easy dollars that supply the year's plain clothing and meals, the melancholy prudence of the abandonment of such a great being as a man is to the toss and pallor of years of moneymaking with all their scorching days and icy nights and all their stifling deceits and underhanded dodgings, or infinitessimals of parlors, or shameless stuffing while others starve . . . and all the loss of the bloom and odor of the earth and of the flowers and atmosphere and of the sea and of the true taste of the women and men you pass or have to do with in youth or middle age, and the issuing sickness and desperate revolt at the close of a life without elevation or naivete, and the ghastly chatter of a death without serenity or majesty, is the great fraud upon modern civilization and forethought, blotching the surface and system which civilization undeniably drafts, and moistening with tears the immense features it spreads and spreads with such velocity before the reached kisses of the soul. . . . Still the right explanation remains to be made about prudence. The prudence of the mere wealth and respectability of the most esteemed life appears too faint for the eye to observe at all when little and large alike drop quietly aside at the thought of the prudence suitable for immortality. What is wisdom that fills the thinness of a year or seventy or eighty years to wisdom spaced out by ages and coming back at a certain time with strong reinforcements and rich presents and the clear faces of wedding-guests as far as you can look in every direction running gaily toward you? Only the soul is of itself . . . all else has reference to what ensues. All that a person does or thinks is of consequence. Not a move can a man or woman make that affects him or her in a day or a month or any part of the direct lifetime or the hour of death but the same affects him or her onward afterward through the indirect lifetime. The indirect is always as great and real as the direct. The spirit receives from the body just as much as it gives to the body. Not one name of word or deed . . . not of venereal sores or discolorations . . . not the privacy of the onanist . . . not of the putrid veins of gluttons or rumdrinkers . . . not peculation or cunning or betrayal or murder . . . no serpentine poison of those that seduce women . . . not the foolish yielding of women . . . not prostitution . . . not of any depravity of young men . . . not of the attainment of gain by discreditable means . . . not any nastiness of appetite . . . not any harshness of officers to men or judges to prisoners or fathers to sons or sons to fathers or of husbands to wives or bosses to their boys . . . not of greedy looks or malignant wishes . . . nor any of the wiles practised by people upon themselves . . . ever is or ever can be stamped on the programme but it is duly realized and returned, and that returned in further performances . . . and they returned again. Nor can the push of charity or personal force ever be any thing else than the profoundest reason, whether it bring arguments to hand or no. No specification is necessary . . . to add or subtract or divide is in vain. Little or big, learned or unlearned, white or black, legal or illegal, sick or well, from the first inspiration down the windpipe to the last expiration out of it, all that a male or female does that is vigorous and benevolent and clean is so much sure profit to him or her in the unshakable order of the universe and through the whole scope of it forever. If the savage or felon is wise it is well . . . if the greatest poet or savan is wise it is simply the same . . . if the President or chief justice is wise it is the same . . . if the young mechanic or farmer is wise it is no more or less . . . if the prostitute is wise it is no more nor less. The interest will come round . . . all will come round. All the best actions of war and peace . . . all help given to relatives and strangers and the poor and old and sorrowful and young children and widows and the sick, and to all shunned persons . . . all furtherance of fugitives and of the escape of slaves . . . all the self-denial that stood steady and aloof on wrecks and saw others take the seats of the boats . . . all offering of substance or life for the good old cause, or for a friend's sake or opinion's sake . . . all pains of enthusiasts scoffed at by their neighbors . . . all the vast sweet love and precious suffering of mothers . . . all honest men baffled in strifes recorded or unrecorded . . . all the grandeur and good of the few ancient nations whose fragments of annals we inherit . . . and all the good of the hundreds of far mightier and more ancient nations unknown to us by name or date or location . . . all that was ever manfully begun, whether it succeeded or no . . . all that has at any time been well suggested out of the divine heart of man or by the divinity of his mouth or by the shaping of his great hands . . . and all that is well thought or done this day on any part of the surface of the globe . . . or on any of the wandering stars or fixed stars by those there as we are here . . . or that is henceforth to be well thought or done by you whoever you are, or by any one—these singly and wholly inured at their time and inure now and will inure always to the identities from which they sprung or shall spring. . . . Did you guess any of them lived only its moment? The world does not so exist . . . no parts palpable or impalpable so exist . . . no result exists now without being from its long antecedent result, and that from its antecedent, and so backward without the farthest mentionable spot coming a bit nearer the beginning than any other spot. . . . Whatever satisfies the soul is truth. The prudence of the greatest poet answers at last the craving and glut of the soul, is not contemptuous of less ways of prudence if they conform to its ways, puts off nothing, permits no let-up for its own case or any case, has no particular sabbath or judgment-day, divides not the living from the dead or the righteous from the unrighteous, is satisfied with the present, matches every thought or act by its correlative, knows no possible forgiveness or deputed atonement . . . knows that the young man who composedly periled his life and lost it has done exceeding well for himself, while the man who has not periled his life and retains it to old age in riches and ease has perhaps achieved nothing for himself worth mentioning . . . and that only that person has no great prudence to learn who has learnt to prefer real longlived things, and favors body and soul the same, and perceives the indirect assuredly following the direct, and what evil or good he does leaping onward and waiting to meet him again—and who in his spirit in any emergency whatever neither hurries or avoids death.

The direct trial of him who would be the greatest poet is today. If he does not flood himself with the immediate age as with vast oceanic tides . . . and if he does not attract his own land body and soul to himself and hang on its neck with incomparable love and plunge his semitic muscle into its merits and demerits . . . and if he be not himself the age transfigured . . . and if to him is not opened the eternity which gives similitude to all periods and locations and processes and animate and inanimate forms, and which is the bond of time, and rises up from its inconceivable vagueness and infiniteness in the swimming shape of today, and is held by the ductile anchors of life, and makes the present spot the passage from what was to what shall be, and commits itself to the representation of this wave of an hour and this one of the sixty beautiful children of the wave—let him merge in the general run and wait his development. . . . Still the final test of poems or any character or work remains. The prescient poet projects himself centuries ahead and judges performer or performance after the changes of time. Does it live through them? Does it still hold on untired? Will the same style and the direction of genius to similar points be satisfactory now? Has no new discovery in science or arrival at superior planes of thought and judgment and behaviour fixed him or his so that either can be looked down upon? Have the marches of tens and hundreds and thousands of years made willing detours to the right hand and the left hand for his sake? Is he beloved long and long after he is buried? Does the young man think often of him? and the young woman think often of him? and do the middleaged and the old think of him?

A great poem is for ages and ages in common and for all degrees and complexions and all departments and sects and for a woman as much as a man and a man as much as a woman. A great poem is no finish to a man or woman but rather a beginning. Has any one fancied he could sit at last under some due authority and rest satisfied with explanations and realize and be content and full? To no such terminus does the greatest poet bring . . . he brings neither cessation or sheltered fatness and ease. The touch of him tells in action. Whom he takes he takes with firm sure grasp into live regions previously unattained . . . thenceforward is no rest . . . they see the space and ineffable sheen that turn the old spots and lights into dead vacuums. The companion of him beholds the birth and progress of stars and learns one of the meanings. Now there shall be a man cohered out of tumult and chaos . . . the elder encourages the younger and shows him how . . . they two shall launch off fearlessly together till the new world fits an orbit for itself and looks unabashed on the lesser orbits of the stars and sweeps through the ceaseless rings and shall never be quiet again.

There will soon be no more priests. Their work is done. They may wait awhile . . . perhaps a generation or two . . . dropping off by degrees. A superior breed shall take their place . . . the gangs of kosmos and prophets en masse shall take their place. A new order shall arise and they shall be the priests of man, and every man shall be his own priest. The churches built under their umbrage shall be the churches of men and women. Through the divinity of themselves shall the kosmos and the new breed of poets be interpreters of men and women and of all events and things. They shall find their inspiration in real objects today, symptoms of the past and future. . . . They shall not deign to defend immortality or God or the perfection of things or liberty or the exquisite beauty and reality of the soul. They shall arise in America and be responded to from the remainder of the earth.

The English language befriends the grand American expression . . . it is brawny enough and limber and full enough. On the tough stock of a race who through all change of circumstance was never without the idea of political liberty, which is the animus of all liberty, it has attracted the terms of daintier and gayer and subtler and more elegant tongues. It is the powerful language of resistance . . . it is the dialect of common sense. It is the speech of the proud and melancholy races and of all who aspire. It is the chosen tongue to express growth faith self-esteem freedom justice equality friendliness amplitude prudence decision and courage. It is the medium that shall well nigh express the inexpressible.

No great literature nor any like style of behaviour or oratory or social intercourse or household arrangements or public institutions or the treatment by bosses of employed people, nor executive detail or detail of the army or navy, nor spirit of legislation or courts or police or tuition or architecture or songs or amusements or the costumes of young men, can long elude the jealous and passionate instinct of American standards. Whether or no the sign appears from the mouths of the people, it throbs a live interrogation in every freeman's and free-woman's heart after that which passes by or this built to remain. Is it uniform with my country? Are its disposals without ignominious distinctions? Is it for the evergrowing communes of brothers and lovers, large, well-united, proud beyond the old models, generous beyond all models? Is it something grown fresh out of the fields or drawn from the sea for use to me today here? I know that what answers for me an American must answer for any individual or nation that serves for a part of my materials. Does this answer? or is it without reference to universal needs? or sprung of the needs of the less developed society of special ranks? or old needs of pleasure overlaid by modern science and forms? Does this acknowledge liberty with audible and absolute acknowledgement, and set slavery at nought for life and death? Will it help breed one goodshaped and wellhung man, and a woman to be his perfect and independent mate? Does it improve manners? Is it for the nursing of the young of the republic? Does it solve readily with the sweet milk of the nipples of the breasts of the mother of many children? Has it too the old ever-fresh forbearance and impartiality? Does it look with the same love on the last born and on those hardening toward stature, and on the errant, and on those who disdain all strength of assault outside of their own?

The poems distilled from other poems will probably pass away. The coward will surely pass away. The expectation of the vital and great can only be satisfied by the demeanor of the vital and great. The swarms of the polished deprecating and reflectors and the polite float off and leave no remembrance. America prepares with composure and goodwill for the visitors that have sent word. It is not intellect that is to be their warrant and welcome. The talented, the artist, the ingenious, the editor, the statesman, the erudite . . . they are not unappreciated . . . they fall in their place and do their work. The soul of the nation also does its work. No disguise can pass on it . . . no disguise can conceal from it. It rejects none, it permits all. Only toward as good as itself and toward the like of itself will it advance half-way. An individual is as superb as a nation when he has the qualities which make a superb nation. The soul of the largest and wealthiest and proudest nation may well go half-way to meet that of its poets. The signs are effectual. There is no fear of mistake. If the one is true the other is true. The proof of a poet is that his country absorbs him as affectionately as he has absorbed it.

LEAVES OF GRASS

ICELEBRATE myself,
And what I assume you shall assume,
For every atom belonging to me as good belongs to you.

I loafe and invite my soul,
I lean and loafe at my ease . . . observing a spear of summer grass.

Houses and rooms are full of perfumes . . . the shelves are crowded
    with perfumes,
I breathe the fragrance myself, and know it and like it,
The distillation would intoxicate me also, but I shall not let it.

The atmosphere is not a perfume . . . it has no taste of the distillation
    . . . it is odorless,
It is for my mouth forever . . . I am in love with it,
I will go to the bank by the wood and become undisguised and naked,
I am mad for it to be in contact with me.

The smoke of my own breath,
Echos, ripples, and buzzed whispers . . . loveroot, silkthread, crotch and
    vine,
My respiration and inspiration . . . the beating of my heart . . . the pass-
    ing of blood and air through my lungs,
The sniff of green leaves and dry leaves, and of the shore and dark-
    colored sea-rocks, and of hay in the barn,
The sound of the belched words of my voice . . . words loosed to the
    eddies of the wind,
A few light kisses . . . a few embraces . . . a reaching around of arms,
The play of shine and shade on the trees as the supple boughs wag,
The delight alone or in the rush of the streets, or along the fields and
    hillsides,
The feeling of health . . . the full-noon trill . . . the song of me rising
    from bed and meeting the sun.

Have you reckoned a thousand acres much? Have you reckoned the
    earth much?
Have you practiced so long to learn to read?
Have you felt so proud to get at the meaning of poems?

Stop this day and night with me and you shall possess the origin of all
    poems,
You shall possess the good of the earth and sun . . . there are millions
    of suns left,
You shall no longer take things at second or third hand . . . nor look
    through the eyes of the dead . . . nor feed on the spectres in
    books,
You shall not look through my eyes either, nor take things from me,
You shall listen to all sides and filter them from yourself.

I have heard what the talkers were talking . . . the talk of the begin-
    ning and the end,
But I do not talk of the beginning or the end.

There was never any more inception than there is now,
Nor any more youth or age than there is now;
And will never be any more perfection than there is now,
Nor any more heaven or hell than there is now.

Urge and urge and urge,
Always the procreant urge of the world.

Out of the dimness opposite equals advance . . . Always substance and
    increase,
Always a knit of identity . . . always distinction . . . always a breed of
    life.

To elaborate is no avail . . . Learned and unlearned feel that it is so.

Sure as the most certain sure . . . plumb in the uprights, well entretied,
    braced in the beams,
Stout as a horse, affectionate, haughty, electrical,
I and this mystery here we stand.

Clear and sweet is my soul . . . and clear and sweet is all that is not my
    soul.

Lack one lacks both . . . and the unseen is proved by the seen,
Till that becomes unseen and receives proof in its turn.

Showing the best and dividing it from the worst, age vexes age,
Knowing the perfect fitness and equanimity of things, while they
    discuss I am silent, and go bathe and admire myself.

Welcome is every organ and attribute of me, and of any man hearty
    and clean,
Not an inch nor a particle of an inch is vile, and none shall be less
    familiar than the rest.

I am satisfied . . . I see, dance, laugh, sing;
As God comes a loving bedfellow and sleeps at my side all night and
    close on the peep of the day,
And leaves for me baskets covered with white towels bulging the
    house with their plenty,
Shall I postpone my acceptation and realization and scream at my eyes,
That they turn from gazing after and down the road,
And forthwith cipher and show me to a cent,
Exactly the contents of one, and exactly the contents of two, and
    which is ahead?

Trippers and askers surround me,
People I meet . . . the effect upon me of my early life . . . of the ward
    and city I live in . . . of the nation,
The latest news . . . discoveries, inventions, societies . . . authors old and
    new,
My dinner, dress, associates, looks, business, compliments, dues,
The real or fancied indifference of some man or woman I love,
The sickness of one of my folks—or of myself . . . or ill-doing . . .
    or loss or lack of money . . . or depressions or exaltations,
They come to me days and nights and go from me again,
But they are not the Me myself.

Apart from the pulling and hauling stands what I am,
Stands amused, complacent, compassionating, idle, unitary,
Looks down, is erect, bends an arm on an impalpable certain rest,
Looks with its sidecurved head curious what will come next,
Both in and out of the game, and watching and wondering at it.

Backward I see in my own days where I sweated through fog with
    linguists and contenders,
I have no mockings or arguments . . . I witness and wait.

I believe in you my soul . . . the other I am must not abase itself to
    you,
And you must not be abased to the other.

Loafe with me on the grass . . . loose the stop from your throat,
Not words, not music or rhyme I want . . . not custom or lecture, not
    even the best,
Only the lull I like, the hum of your valved voice.

I mind how we lay in June, such a transparent summer morning;
You settled your head athwart my hips and gently turned over upon
    me,
And parted the shirt from my bosom-bone, and plunged your tongue
    to my barestript heart,
And reached till you felt my beard, and reached till you held my feet.

Swiftly arose and spread around me the peace and joy and knowledge
    that pass all the art and argument of the earth;
And I know that the hand of God is the elderhand of my own,
And I know that the spirit of God is the eldest brother of my own,
And that all the men ever born are also my brothers . . . and the
    women my sisters and lovers,
And that a kelson of the creation is love;
And limitless are leaves stiff or drooping in the fields,
And brown ants in the little wells beneath them,
And mossy scabs of the wormfence, and heaped stones, and elder and
    mullen and pokeweed.

A child said, What is the grass? fetching it to me with full hands;
How could I answer the child? . . . I do not know what it is any more
    than he.

I guess it must be the flag of my disposition, out of hopeful green stuff
    woven.

Or I guess it is the handkerchief of the Lord,
A scented gift and remembrancer designedly dropped,
Bearing the owner's name someway in the corners, that we may see
    and remark, and say Whose?

Or I guess the grass is itself a child . . . the produced babe of the
    vegetation.

Or I guess it is a uniform hieroglyphic,
And it means, Sprouting alike in broad zones and narrow zones,
Growing among black folks as among white,
Kanuck, Tuckahoe, Congressman, Cuff, I give them the same, I
    receive them the same.

And now it seems to me the beautiful uncut hair of graves.

Tenderly will I use you curling grass,
It may be you transpire from the breasts of young men,
It may be if I had known them I would have loved them;
It may be you are from old people and from women, and from
    offspring taken soon out of their mothers' laps,

And here you are the mothers' laps.

This grass is very dark to be from the white heads of old mothers,
Darker than the colorless beards of old men,
Dark to come from under the faint red roofs of mouths.

O I perceive after all so many uttering tongues!
And I perceive they do not come from the roofs of mouths for
    nothing.

I wish I could translate the hints about the dead young men and
    women,
And the hints about old men and mothers, and the offspring taken
    soon out of their laps.

What do you think has become of the young and old men?
And what do you think has become of the women and children?

They are alive and well somewhere;
The smallest sprout shows there is really no death,
And if ever there was it led forward life, and does not wait at the end
    to arrest it,
And ceased the moment life appeared.

All goes onward and outward . . . and nothing collapses,
And to die is different from what any one supposed, and luckier.

Has any one supposed it lucky to be born?
I hasten to inform him or her it is just as lucky to die, and I know it.

I pass death with the dying, and birth with the new-washed babe . . .
    and am not contained between my hat and boots,
And peruse manifold objects, no two alike, and every one good,
The earth good, and the stars good, and their adjuncts all good.

I am not an earth nor an adjunct of an earth,
I am the mate and companion of people, all just as immortal and
    fathomless as myself;
They do not know how immortal, but I know.

Every kind for itself and its own . . . for me mine male and female,
For me all that have been boys and that love women,
For me the man that is proud and feels how it stings to be slighted,
For me the sweetheart and the old maid . . . for me mothers and the
    mothers of mothers,
For me lips that have smiled, eyes that have shed tears,
For me children and the begetters of children.

Who need be afraid of the merge?
Undrape . . . you are not guilty to me, nor stale nor discarded,
I see through the broadcloth and gingham whether or no,
And am around, tenacious, acquisitive, tireless . . . and can never be
    shaken away.

The little one sleeps in its cradle,
I lift the gauze and look a long time, and silently brush away flies with
    my hand.

The youngster and the redfaced girl turn aside up the bushy hill,
I peeringly view them from the top.

The suicide sprawls on the bloody floor of the bedroom.
It is so . . . I witnessed the corpse . . . there the pistol had fallen.

The blab of the pave . . . the tires of carts and sluff of bootsoles and
    talk of the promenaders,
The heavy omnibus, the driver with his interrogating thumb, the
    clank of the shod horses on the granite floor,
The carnival of sleighs, the clinking and shouted jokes and pelts of
    snowballs;
The hurrahs for popular favorites . . . the fury of roused mobs,
The flap of the curtained litter—the sick man inside, borne to the
    hospital,
The meeting of enemies, the sudden oath, the blows and fall,
The excited crowd—the policeman with his star quickly working his
    passage to the centre of the crowd;
The impassive stones that receive and return so many echoes,
The souls moving along . . . are they invisible while the least atom of
    the stones is visible?
What groans of overfed or half-starved who fall on the flags sunstruck
    or in fits,
What exclamations of women taken suddenly, who hurry home and
    give birth to babes,
What living and buried speech is always vibrating here . . . what howls
    restrained by decorum,
Arrests of criminals, slights, adulterous offers made, acceptances,
    rejections with convex lips,
I mind them or the resonance of them . . . I come again and again.

The big doors of the country-barn stand open and ready,
The dried grass of the harvest-time loads the slow-drawn wagon,
The clear light plays on the brown gray and green intertinged,
The armfuls are packed to the sagging mow:

I am there . . . I help . . . I came stretched atop of the load,
I felt its soft jolts . . . one leg reclined on the other,
I jump from the crossbeams, and seize the clover and timothy,
And roll head over heels, and tangle my hair full of wisps.

Alone far in the wilds and mountains I hunt,
Wandering amazed at my own lightness and glee,
In the late afternoon choosing a safe spot to pass the night,
Kindling a fire and broiling the freshkilled game,
Soundly falling asleep on the gathered leaves, my dog and gun by my
    side.

The Yankee clipper is under her three skysails . . . she cuts the sparkle
    and scud,
My eyes settle the land . . . I bend at her prow or shout joyously from
    the deck.

The boatmen and clamdiggers arose early and stopped for me,
I tucked my trowser-ends in my boots and went and had a good time,
You should have been with us that day round the chowder-kettle.

I saw the marriage of the trapper in the open air in the far-west . . .
    the bride was a red girl,
Her father and his friends sat near by crosslegged and dumbly smok-
    ing . . . they had moccasins to their feet and large thick blankets
    hanging from their shoulders;
On a bank lounged the trapper . . . he was dressed mostly in skins . . .
    his luxuriant beard and curls protected his neck,
One hand rested on his rifle . . . the other hand held firmly the wrist
    of the red girl,
She had long eyelashes . . . her head was bare . . . her coarse straight
    locks descended upon her voluptuous limbs and reached to her
    feet.

The runaway slave came to my house and stopped outside,
I heard his motions crackling the twigs of the woodpile,
Through the swung half-door of the kitchen I saw him limpsey and
    weak,
And went where he sat on a log, and led him in and assured him,
And brought water and filled a tub for his sweated body and bruised
    feet,
And gave him a room that entered from my own, and gave him some
    coarse clean clothes,
And remember perfectly well his revolving eyes and his awkwardness,
And remember putting plasters on the galls of his neck and ankles;

He staid with me a week before he was recuperated and passed north,
I had him sit next me at table . . . my firelock leaned in the corner.

Twenty-eight young men bathe by the shore,
Twenty-eight young men, and all so friendly,
Twenty-eight years of womanly life, and all so lonesome.

She owns the fine house by the rise of the bank,
She hides handsome and richly drest aft the blinds of the window.

Which of the young men does she like the best?
Ah the homeliest of them is beautiful to her.

Where are you off to, lady? for I see you,
You splash in the water there, yet stay stock still in your room.

Dancing and laughing along the beach came the twenty-ninth bather,
The rest did not see her, but she saw them and loved them.

The beards of the young men glistened with wet, it ran from their
       long hair,
Little streams passed all over their bodies.

An unseen hand also passed over their bodies,
It descended tremblingly from their temples and ribs.

The young men float on their backs, their white bellies swell to the
       sun . . . they do not ask who seizes fast to them,
They do not know who puffs and declines with pendant and bending
       arch,
They do not think whom they souse with spray.

The butcher-boy puts off his killing-clothes, or sharpens his knife at
       the stall in the market,
I loiter enjoying his repartee and his shuffle and breakdown.

Blacksmiths with grimed and hairy chests environ the anvil,
Each has his main-sledge . . . they are all out . . . there is a great heat
       in the fire.

From the cinder-strewed threshold I follow their movements,
The lithe sheer of their waists plays even with their massive arms,
Overhand the hammers roll—overhand so slow—overhand so sure,
They do not hasten, each man hits in his place.

The negro holds firmly the reins of his four horses . . . the block swags
       underneath on its tied-over chain,
The negro that drives the huge dray of the stoneyard . . . steady and
       tall he stands poised on one leg on the stringpiece,

His blue shirt exposes his ample neck and breast and loosens over his
hipband,
His glance is calm and commanding . . . he tosses the slouch of his hat
away from his forehead,
The sun falls on his crispy hair and moustache . . . falls on the black
of his polish'd and perfect limbs.

I behold the picturesque giant and love him . . . and I do not stop
there,
I go with the team also.

In me the caresser of life wherever moving . . . backward as well as
forward slueing,
To niches aside and junior bending.

Oxen that rattle the yoke or halt in the shade, what is that you express
in your eyes?
It seems to me more than all the print I have read in my life.

My tread scares the wood-drake and wood-duck on my distant and
daylong ramble,
They rise together, they slowly circle around.
. . . I believe in those winged purposes,
And acknowledge the red yellow and white playing within me,
And consider the green and violet and the tufted crown intentional;
And do not call the tortoise unworthy because she is not something
else,
And the mockingbird in the swamp never studied the gamut, yet trills
pretty well to me,
And the look of the bay mare shames silliness out of me.

The wild gander leads his flock through the cool night,
Ya-honk! he says, and sounds it down to me like an invitation;
The pert may suppose it meaningless, but I listen closer,
I find its purpose and place up there toward the November sky.

The sharphoofed moose of the north, the cat on the housesill, the
chickadee, the prairie-dog,
The litter of the grunting sow as they tug at her teats,
The brood of the turkeyhen, and she with her halfspread wings,
I see in them and myself the same old law.

The press of my foot to the earth springs a hundred affections,
They scorn the best I can do to relate them.

I am enamoured of growing outdoors,
Of men that live among cattle or taste of the ocean or woods,

Of the builders and steerers of ships, of the wielders of axes and
    mauls, of the drivers of horses,
I can eat and sleep with them week in and week out.

What is commonest and cheapest and nearest and easiest is Me,
Me going in for my chances, spending for vast returns,
Adorning myself to bestow myself on the first that will take me,
Not asking the sky to come down to my goodwill,
Scattering it freely forever.

The pure contralto sings in the organloft,
The carpenter dresses his plank . . . the tongue of his foreplane
    whistles its wild ascending lisp,
The married and unmarried children ride home to their thanksgiving
    dinner,
The pilot seizes the king-pin, he heaves down with a strong arm,
The mate stands braced in the whaleboat, lance and harpoon are
    ready,
The duck-shooter walks by silent and cautious stretches,
The deacons are ordained with crossed hands at the altar,
The spinning-girl retreats and advances to the hum of the big wheel,
The farmer stops by the bars of a Sunday and looks at the oats and
    rye,
The lunatic is carried at last to the asylum a confirmed case,
He will never sleep any more as he did in the cot in his mother's
    bedroom;
The jour printer with gray head and gaunt jaws works at his case,
He turns his quid of tobacco, his eyes get blurred with the manuscript;
The malformed limbs are tied to the anatomist's table,
What is removed drops horribly in a pail;
The quadroon girl is sold at the stand . . . the drunkard nods by the
    barroom stove,
The machinist rolls up his sleeves . . . the policeman travels his beat . . .
    the gate-keeper marks who pass,
The young fellow drives the express-wagon . . . I love him though I
    do not know him;
The half-breed straps on his light boots to compete in the race,
The western turkey-shooting draws old and young . . . some lean on
    their rifles, some sit on logs,
Out from the crowd steps the marksman and takes his position and
    levels his piece;
The groups of newly-come immigrants cover the wharf or levee,
The woollypates hoe in the sugarfield, the overseer views them from
    his saddle;

The bugle calls in the ballroom, the gentlemen run for their partners, the dancers bow to each other;

The youth lies awake in the cedar-roofed garret and harks to the musical rain,

The Wolverine sets traps on the creek that helps fill the Huron,

The reformer ascends the platform, he spouts with his mouth and nose,

The company returns from its excursion, the darkey brings up the rear and bears the well-riddled target,

The squaw wrapt in her yellow-hemmed cloth is offering moccasins and beadbags for sale,

The connoisseur peers along the exhibition-gallery with halfshut eyes bent sideways,

The deckhands make fast the steamboat, the plank is thrown for the shoregoing passengers,

The young sister holds out the skein, the elder sister winds it off in a ball and stops now and then for the knots,

The one-year wife is recovering and happy, a week ago she bore her first child,

The cleanhaired Yankee girl works with her sewing-machine or in the factory or mill,

The nine months' gone is in the parturition chamber, her faintness and pains are advancing;

The pavingman leans on his twohanded rammer—the reporter's lead flies swiftly over the notebook—the signpainter is lettering with red and gold,

The canal-boy trots on the towpath—the bookkeeper counts at his desk—the shoemaker waxes his thread,

The conductor beats time for the band and all the performers follow him,

The child is baptised—the convert is making the first professions,

The regatta is spread on the bay . . . how the white sails sparkle!

The drover watches his drove, he sings out to them that would stray,

The pedlar sweats with his pack on his back—the purchaser higgles about the odd cent,

The camera and plate are prepared, the lady must sit for her daguerreotype,

The bride unrumples her white dress, the minutehand of the clock moves slowly,

The opium eater reclines with rigid head and just-opened lips,

The prostitute draggles her shawl, her bonnet bobs on her tipsy and pimpled neck,

The crowd laugh at her blackguard oaths, the men jeer and wink to each other,

(Miserable! I do not laugh at your oaths nor jeer you,)
The President holds a cabinet council, he is surrounded by the great
    secretaries,
On the piazza walk five friendly matrons with twined arms;
The crew of the fish-smack pack repeated layers of halibut in the
    hold,
The Missourian crosses the plains toting his wares and his cattle,
The fare-collector goes through the train—he gives notice by the jin-
    gling of loose change,
The floormen are laying the floor—the tinners are tinning the roof—
    the masons are calling for mortar,
In single file each shouldering his hod pass onward the laborers;
Seasons pursuing each other the indescribable crowd is gathered . . .
    it is the Fourth of July . . . what salutes of cannon and small arms!
Seasons pursuing each other the plougher ploughs and the mower
    mows and the wintergrain falls in the ground;
Off on the lakes the pikefisher watches and waits by the hole in the
    frozen surface,
The stumps stand thick round the clearing, the squatter strikes deep
    with his axe,
The flatboatmen make fast toward dusk near the cottonwood or
    pekantrees,
The coon-seekers go now through the regions of the Red river, or
    through those drained by the Tennessee, or through those of the
    Arkansas,
The torches shine in the dark that hangs on the Chattahoochee or
    Altamahaw;
Patriarchs sit at supper with sons and grandsons and great grandsons
    around them,
In walls of adobe, in canvass tents, rest hunters and trappers after their
    day's sport.
The city sleeps and the country sleeps,
The living sleep for their time . . . the dead sleep for their time,
The old husband sleeps by his wife and the young husband sleeps by
    his wife;
And these one and all tend inward to me, and I tend outward to them,
And such as it is to be of these more or less I am.

I am of old and young, of the foolish as much as the wise,
Regardless of others, ever regardful of others,
Maternal as well as paternal, a child as well as a man,
Stuffed with the stuff that is coarse, and stuffed with the stuff that is
    fine,

One of the great nation, the nation of many nations—the smallest the
    same and the largest the same,
A southerner soon as a northerner, a planter nonchalant and
    hospitable,
A Yankee bound my own way . . . ready for trade . . . my joints the
    limberest joints on earth and the sternest joints on earth,
A Kentuckian walking the vale of the Elkhorn in my deerskin
    leggings,
A boatman over the lakes or bays or along coasts . . . a Hoosier,
    a Badger, a Buckeye,
A Louisianian or Georgian, a poke-easy from sandhills and pines,
At home on Canadian snowshoes or up in the bush, or with fisher-
    men off Newfoundland,
At home in the fleet of iceboats, sailing with the rest and tacking,
At home on the hills of Vermont or in the woods of Maine or the
    Texan ranch,
Comrade of Californians . . . comrade of free northwesterners, loving
    their big proportions,
Comrade of raftsmen and coalmen—comrade of all who shake hands
    and welcome to drink and meat;
A learner with the simplest, a teacher of the thoughtfulest,
A novice beginning experient of myriads of seasons,
Of every hue and trade and rank, of every caste and religion,
Not merely of the New World but of Africa Europe or Asia . . .
    a wandering savage,
A farmer, mechanic, or artist . . . a gentleman, sailor, lover or quaker,
A prisoner, fancy-man, rowdy, lawyer, physician or priest.

I resist anything better than my own diversity,
And breathe the air and leave plenty after me,
And am not stuck up, and am in my place.

The moth and the fisheggs are in their place,
The suns I see and the suns I cannot see are in their place,
The palpable is in its place and the impalpable is in its place.

These are the thoughts of all men in all ages and lands, they are not
    original with me,
If they are not yours as much as mine they are nothing or next to
    nothing,
If they do not enclose everything they are next to nothing,
If they are not the riddle and the untying of the riddle they are
    nothing,
If they are not just as close as they are distant they are nothing.

This is the grass that grows wherever the land is and the water is,
This is the common air that bathes the globe.

This is the breath of laws and songs and behaviour,
This is the tasteless water of souls . . . this is the true sustenance,
It is for the illiterate . . . it is for the judges of the supreme court . . .
  it is for the federal capitol and the state capitols,
It is for the admirable communes of literary men and composers and
  singers and lecturers and engineers and savans,
It is for the endless races of working people and farmers and seamen.

This is the trill of a thousand clear cornets and scream of the octave
  flute and strike of triangles.

I play not a march for victors only . . . I play great marches for con-
  quered and slain persons.

Have you heard that it was good to gain the day?
I also say it is good to fall . . . battles are lost in the same spirit in which
  they are won.

I sound triumphal drums for the dead . . . I fling through my
  embouchures the loudest and gayest music to them,
Vivas to those who have failed, and to those whose war-vessels sank
  in the sea, and those themselves who sank in the sea,
And to all generals that lost engagements, and all overcome heroes,
  and the numberless unknown heroes equal to the greatest heroes
  known.

This is the meal pleasantly set . . . this is the meat and drink for natural
  hunger,
It is for the wicked just the same as the righteous . . . I make appoint-
  ments with all,
I will not have a single person slighted or left away,
The keptwoman and sponger and thief are hereby invited . . . the
  heavy-lipped slave is invited . . . the venerealee is invited,
There shall be no difference between them and the rest.

This is the press of a bashful hand . . . this is the float and odor of hair,
This is the touch of my lips to yours . . . this is the murmur of
  yearning,
This is the far-off depth and height reflecting my own face,
This is the thoughtful merge of myself and the outlet again.

Do you guess I have some intricate purpose?
Well I have . . . for the April rain has, and the mica on the side of a
  rock has.

Do you take it I would astonish?
Does the daylight astonish? or the early redstart twittering through the
    woods?
Do I astonish more than they?

This hour I tell things in confidence,
I might not tell everybody but I will tell you.

Who goes there! hankering, gross, mystical, nude?
How is it I extract strength from the beef I eat?

What is a man anyhow? What am I? and what are you?
All I mark as my own you shall offset it with your own,
Else it were time lost listening to me.

I do not snivel that snivel the world over,
That months are vacuums and the ground but wallow and filth,
That life is a suck and a sell, and nothing remains at the end but
    threadbare crape and tears.

Whimpering and truckling fold with powders for invalids ... confor-
    mity goes to the fourth-removed,
I cock my hat as I please indoors or out.

Shall I pray? Shall I venerate and be ceremonious?

I have pried through the strata and analyzed to a hair,
And counselled with doctors and calculated close and found no
    sweeter fat than sticks to my own bones.

In all people I see myself, none more and not one a barleycorn less,
And the good or bad I say of myself I say of them.

And I know I am solid and sound,
To me the converging objects of the universe perpetually flow,
All are written to me, and I must get what the writing means.

And I know I am deathless,
I know this orbit of mine cannot be swept by a carpenter's compass,
I know I shall not pass like a child's carlacue cut with a burnt stick at
    night.

I know I am august,
I do not trouble my spirit to vindicate itself or be understood,
I see that the elementary laws never apologize,
I reckon I behave no prouder than the level I plant my house by after
    all.

I exist as I am, that is enough,

If no other in the world be aware I sit content,
And if each and all be aware I sit content.

One world is aware, and by far the largest to me, and that is myself,
And whether I come to my own today or in ten thousand or ten
    million years,
I can cheerfully take it now, or with equal cheerfulness I can wait.

My foothold is tenoned and mortised in granite,
I laugh at what you call dissolution,
And I know the amplitude of time.

I am the poet of the body,
And I am the poet of the soul.

The pleasures of heaven are with me, and the pains of hell are with
    me,
The first I graft and increase upon myself . . . the latter I translate into
    a new tongue.

I am the poet of the woman the same as the man,
And I say it is as great to be a woman as to be a man,
And I say there is nothing greater than the mother of men.

I chant a new chant of dilation or pride,
We have had ducking and deprecating about enough,
I show that size is only developement.

Have you outstript the rest? Are you the President?
It is a trifle . . . they will more than arrive there every one, and still
    pass on.

I am he that walks with the tender and growing night;
I call to the earth and sea half-held by the night.

Press close barebosomed night! Press close magnetic nourishing night!
Night of south winds! Night of the large few stars!
Still nodding night! Mad naked summer night!

Smile O voluptuous coolbreathed earth!
Earth of the slumbering and liquid trees!
Earth of departed sunset! Earth of the mountains misty-topt!
Earth of the vitreous pour of the full moon just tinged with blue!
Earth of shine and dark mottling the tide of the river!
Earth of the limpid gray of clouds brighter and clearer for my sake!
Far-swooping elbowed earth! Rich apple-blossomed earth!
Smile, for your lover comes!

Prodigal! you have given me love! . . . therefore I to you give love!
O unspeakable passionate love!

Thruster holding me tight and that I hold tight!
We hurt each other as the bridegroom and the bride hurt each other.

You sea! I resign myself to you also . . . I guess what you mean,
I behold from the beach your crooked inviting fingers,
I believe you refuse to go back without feeling of me;
We must have a turn together . . . I undress . . . hurry me out of sight
     of the land,
Cushion me soft . . . rock me in billowy drowse,
Dash me with amorous wet . . . I can repay you.

Sea of stretched ground-swells!
Sea breathing broad and convulsive breaths!
Sea of the brine of life! Sea of unshovelled and always-ready graves!
Howler and scooper of storms! Capricious and dainty sea!
I am integral with you . . . I too am of one phase and of all phases.

Partaker of influx and efflux . . . extoler of hate and conciliation,
Extoler of amies and those that sleep in each others' arms.

I am he attesting sympathy;
Shall I make my list of things in the house and skip the house that
     supports them?

I am the poet of commonsense and of the demonstrable and of
     immortality;
And am not the poet of goodness only . . . I do not decline to be the
     poet of wickedness also.

Washes and razors for foofoos . . . for me freckles and a bristling beard.

What blurt is it about virtue and about vice?
Evil propels me, and reform of evil propels me . . . I stand indifferent,
My gait is no faultfinder's or rejecter's gait,
I moisten the roots of all that has grown.

Did you fear some scrofula out of the unflagging pregnancy?
Did you guess the celestial laws are yet to be worked over and
     rectified?

I step up to say that what we do is right and what we affirm is right
     . . . and some is only the ore of right,
Witnesses of us . . . one side a balance and the antipodal side a balance,
Soft doctrine as steady help as stable doctrine,
Thoughts and deeds of the present our rouse and early start.

This minute that comes to me over the past decillions,
There is no better than it and now.

What behaved well in the past or behaves well today is not such a
    wonder,
The wonder is always and always how there can be a mean man or an
    infidel.

Endless unfolding of words of ages!
And mine a word of the modern . . . a word en masse.

A word of the faith that never balks,
One time as good as another time . . . here or henceforward it is all
    the same to me.

A word of reality . . . materialism first and last imbueing.

Hurrah for positive science! Long live exact demonstration!
Fetch stonecrop and mix it with cedar and branches of lilac;
This is the lexicographer or chemist . . . this made a grammar of the
    old cartouches,
These mariners put the ship through dangerous unknown seas,
This is the geologist, and this works with the scalpel, and this is a
    mathematician.

Gentlemen I receive you, and attach and clasp hands with you,
The facts are useful and real . . . they are not my dwelling . . . I enter
    by them to an area of the dwelling.

I am less the reminder of property or qualities, and more the reminder
    of life,
And go on the square for my own sake and for others' sakes,
And make short account of neuters and geldings, and favor men and
    women fully equipped,
And beat the gong of revolt, and stop with fugitives and them that
    plot and conspire.

Walt Whitman, an American, one of the roughs, a kosmos,
Disorderly fleshy and sensual . . . eating drinking and breeding,
No sentimentalist . . . no stander above men and women or apart from
    them . . . no more modest than immodest.

Unscrew the locks from the doors!
Unscrew the doors themselves from their jambs!

Whoever degrades another degrades me . . . and whatever is done or
    said returns at last to me,
And whatever I do or say I also return.

Through me the afflatus surging and surging . . . through me the
  current and index.

I speak the password primeval . . . I give the sign of democracy;
By God! I will accept nothing which all cannot have their counter-
  part of on the same terms.

Through me many long dumb voices,
Voices of the interminable generations of slaves,
Voices of prostitutes and of deformed persons,
Voices of the diseased and despairing, and of thieves and dwarfs,
Voices of cycles of preparation and accretion,
And of the threads that connect the stars—and of wombs, and of the
  fatherstuff,
And of the rights of them the others are down upon,
Of the trivial and flat and foolish and despised,
Of fog in the air and beetles rolling balls of dung.

Through me forbidden voices,
Voices of sexes and lusts . . . voices veiled, and I remove the veil,
Voices indecent by me clarified and transfigured.

I do not press my finger across my mouth,
I keep as delicate around the bowels as around the head and heart,
Copulation is no more rank to me than death is.

I believe in the flesh and the appetites,
Seeing hearing and feeling are miracles, and each part and tag of me
  is a miracle.

Divine am I inside and out, and I make holy whatever I touch or am
  touched from;
The scent of these arm-pits is aroma finer than prayer,
This head is more than churches or bibles or creeds.

If I worship any particular thing it shall be some of the spread of my
  body;
Translucent mould of me it shall be you,
Shaded ledges and rests, firm masculine coulter, it shall be you,
Whatever goes to the tilth of me it shall be you,
You my rich blood, your milky stream pale strippings of my life;
Breast that presses against other breasts it shall be you,
My brain it shall be your occult convolutions,
Root of washed sweet-flag, timorous pond-snipe, nest of guarded
  duplicate eggs, it shall be you,
Mixed tussled hay of head and beard and brawn it shall be you,

Trickling sap of maple, fibre of manly wheat, it shall be you;
Sun so generous it shall be you,
Vapors lighting and shading my face it shall be you,
You sweaty brooks and dews it shall be you,
Winds whose soft-tickling genitals rub against me it shall be you,
Broad muscular fields, branches of liveoak, loving lounger in my
     winding paths, it shall be you,
Hands I have taken, face I have kissed, mortal I have ever touched,
     it shall be you.

I dote on myself . . . there is that lot of me, and all so luscious,
Each moment and whatever happens thrills me with joy.

I cannot tell how my ankles bend . . . nor whence the cause of my
     faintest wish,
Nor the cause of the friendship I emit . . . nor the cause of the friend-
     ship I take again.

To walk up my stoop is unaccountable . . . . I pause to consider if it
     really be,
That I eat and drink is spectacle enough for the great authors and schools,
A morning-glory at my window satisfies me more than the meta-
     physics of books.

To behold the daybreak!
The little light fades the immense and diaphanous shadows,
The air tastes good to my palate.

Hefts of the moving world at innocent gambols, silently rising, freshly
     exuding,
Scooting obliquely high and low.

Something I cannot see puts upward libidinous prongs,
Seas of bright juice suffuse heaven.

The earth by the sky staid with . . . the daily close of their junction,
The heaved challenge from the east that moment over my head,
The mocking taunt, See then whether you shall be master!

Dazzling and tremendous how quick the sunrise would kill me,
If I could not now and always send sunrise out of me.

We also ascend dazzling and tremendous as the sun,
We found our own my soul in the calm and cool of the daybreak.

My voice goes after what my eyes cannot reach,
With the twirl of my tongue I encompass worlds and volumes of
     worlds.

Speech is the twin of my vision . . . it is unequal to measure itself.

It provokes me forever,
It says sarcastically, Walt, you understand enough . . . why don't you let
it out then?

Come now I will not be tantalized . . . you conceive too much of
articulation.

Do you not know how the buds beneath are folded?
Waiting in gloom protected by frost,
The dirt receding before my prophetical screams,
I underlying causes to balance them at last,
My knowledge my live parts . . . it keeping tally with the meaning of
things,
Happiness . . . which whoever hears me let him or her set out in search
of this day.

My final merit I refuse you . . . I refuse putting from me the best I am.

Encompass worlds but never try to encompass me,
I crowd your noisiest talk by looking toward you.

Writing and talk do not prove me,
I carry the plenum of proof and every thing else in my face,
With the hush of my lips I confound the topmost skeptic.

I think I will do nothing for a long time but listen,
And accrue what I hear into myself . . . and let sounds contribute
toward me.

I hear the bravuras of birds . . . the bustle of growing wheat . . . gossip
of flames . . . clack of sticks cooking my meals.

I hear the sound of the human voice . . . a sound I love,
I hear all sounds as they are tuned to their uses . . . sounds of the city
and sounds out of the city . . . sounds of the day and night;
Talkative young ones to those that like them . . . the recitative of fish-
pedlars and fruit-pedlars . . . the loud laugh of workpeople at
their meals,
The angry base of disjointed friendship . . . the faint tones of the sick,
The judge with hands tight to the desk, his shaky lips pronouncing a
death-sentence,
The heave'e'yo of stevedores unlading ships by the wharves . . . the
refrain of the anchor-lifters;
The ring of alarm-bells . . . the cry of fire . . . the whirr of swift-streaking
engines and hose-carts with premonitory tinkles and colored lights,

The steam-whistle . . . the solid roll of the train of approaching cars;
The slow-march played at night at the head of the association,
They go to guard some corpse . . . the flag-tops are draped with black
    muslin.

I hear the violincello or man's heart's complaint,
And hear the keyed cornet or else the echo of sunset.

I hear the chorus . . . it is a grand-opera . . . this indeed is music!

A tenor large and fresh as the creation fills me,
The orbic flex of his mouth is pouring and filling me full.

I hear the trained soprano . . . she convulses me like the climax of my
    love-grip;
The orchestra whirls me wider than Uranus flies,
It wrenches unnamable ardors from my breast,
It throbs me to gulps of the farthest down horror,
It sails me . . . I dab with bare feet . . . they are licked by the indolent
    waves,
I am exposed . . . cut by bitter and poisoned hail,
Steeped amid honeyed morphine . . . my windpipe squeezed in the
    fakes of death,
Let up again to feel the puzzle of puzzles,
And that we call Being.

To be in any form, what is that?
If nothing lay more developed the quahaug and its callous shell were
    enough.

Mine is no callous shell,
I have instant conductors all over me whether I pass or stop,
They seize every object and lead it harmlessly through me.

I merely stir, press, feel with my fingers, and am happy,
To touch my person to some one else's is about as much as I can stand.

Is this then a touch? . . . quivering me to a new identity,
Flames and ether making a rush for my veins,
Treacherous tip of me reaching and crowding to help them,
My flesh and blood playing out lightning, to strike what is hardly
    different from myself,
On all sides prurient provokers stiffening my limbs,
Straining the udder of my heart for its withheld drip,
Behaving licentious toward me, taking no denial,
Depriving me of my best as for a purpose,
Unbuttoning my clothes and holding me by the bare waist,

Deluding my confusion with the calm of the sunlight and pasture
    fields,
Immodestly sliding the fellow-senses away,
They bribed to swap off with touch, and go and graze at the edges
    of me,
No consideration, no regard for my draining strength or my anger,
Fetching the rest of the herd around to enjoy them awhile,
Then all uniting to stand on a headland and worry me.

The sentries desert every other part of me,
They have left me helpless to a red marauder,
They all come to the headland to witness and assist against me.

I am given up by traitors;
I talk wildly . . . I have lost my wits . . . I and nobody else am the great-
    est traitor,
I went myself first to the headland . . . my own hands carried me there.

You villain touch! what are you doing? . . . my breath is tight in its
    throat;
Unclench your floodgates! you are too much for me.

Blind loving wrestling touch! Sheathed hooded sharptoothed touch!
Did it make you ache so leaving me?

Parting tracked by arriving . . . perpetual payment of the perpetual
    loan,
Rich showering rain, and recompense richer afterward.

Sprouts take and accumulate . . . stand by the curb prolific and vital,
Landscapes projected masculine full-sized and golden.

All truths wait in all things,
They neither hasten their own delivery nor resist it,
They do not need the obstetric forceps of the surgeon,
The insignificant is as big to me as any,
What is less or more than a touch?

Logic and sermons never convince,
The damp of the night drives deeper into my soul.

Only what proves itself to every man and woman is so,
Only what nobody denies is so.

A minute and a drop of me settle my brain;
I believe the soggy clods shall become lovers and lamps,
And a compend of compends is the meat of a man or woman,
And a summit and flower there is the feeling they have for each other,

And they are to branch boundlessly out of that lesson until it becomes
omnific,
And until every one shall delight us, and we them.

I believe a leaf of grass is no less than the journeywork of the stars,
And the pismire is equally perfect, and a grain of sand, and the egg of
the wren,
And the tree-toad is a chef-d'ouvre for the highest,
And the running blackberry would adorn the parlors of heaven,
And the narrowest hinge in my hand puts to scorn all machinery,
And the cow crunching with depressed head surpasses any statue,
And a mouse is miracle enough to stagger sextillions of infidels,
And I could come every afternoon of my life to look at the farmer's
girl boiling her iron tea-kettle and baking shortcake.

I find I incorporate gneiss and coal and long-threaded moss and fruits
and grains and esculent roots,
And am stucco'd with quadrupeds and birds all over,
And have distanced what is behind me for good reasons,
And call any thing close again when I desire it.

In vain the speeding or shyness,
In vain the plutonic rocks send their old heat against my approach,
In vain the mastadon retreats beneath its own powdered bones,
In vain objects stand leagues off and assume manifold shapes,
In vain the ocean settling in hollows and the great monsters lying low,
In vain the buzzard houses herself with the sky,
In vain the snake slides through the creepers and logs,
In vain the elk takes to the inner passes of the woods,
In vain the razorbilled auk sails far north to Labrador,
I follow quickly . . . I ascend to the nest in the fissure of the cliff.

I think I could turn and live awhile with the animals . . . they are so
placid and self-contained,
I stand and look at them sometimes half the day long.

They do not sweat and whine about their condition,
They do not lie awake in the dark and weep for their sins,
They do not make me sick discussing their duty to God,
Not one is dissatisfied . . . not one is demented with the mania of
owning things,
Not one kneels to another nor to his kind that lived thousands of
years ago,
Not one is respectable or industrious over the whole earth.

So they show their relations to me and I accept them;

They bring me tokens of myself . . . they evince them plainly in their
    possession.

I do not know where they got those tokens,
I must have passed that way untold times ago and negligently dropt
    them,
Myself moving forward then and now and forever,
Gathering and showing more always and with velocity,
Infinite and omnigenous and the like of these among them;
Not too exclusive toward the reachers of my remembrancers,
Picking out here one that shall be my amie,
Choosing to go with him on brotherly terms.

A gigantic beauty of a stallion, fresh and responsive to my caresses,
Head high in the forehead and wide between the ears,
Limbs glossy and supple, tail dusting the ground,
Eyes well apart and full of sparkling wickedness . . . ears finely cut and
    flexibly moving.

His nostrils dilate . . . my heels embrace him . . . his well built limbs
    tremble with pleasure . . . we speed around and return.

I but use you a moment and then I resign you stallion . . . and do not
    need your paces, and outgallop them,
And myself as I stand or sit pass faster than you.

Swift wind! Space! My Soul! Now I know it is true what I guessed at;
What I guessed when I loafed on the grass,
What I guessed while I lay alone in my bed . . . and again as I walked
    the beach under the paling stars of the morning.

My ties and ballasts leave me . . . I travel . . . I sail . . . my elbows rest
    in the sea-gaps,
I skirt the sierras . . . my palms cover continents,
I am afoot with my vision.

By the city's quadrangular houses . . . in log-huts, or camping with
    lumbermen,
Along the ruts of the turnpike . . . along the dry gulch and rivulet bed,
Hoeing my onion-patch, and rows of carrots and parsnips . . . crossing
    savannas . . . trailing in forests,
Prospecting . . . gold-digging . . . girdling the trees of a new purchase,
Scorched ankle-deep by the hot sand . . . hauling my boat down the
    shallow river;
Where the panther walks to and fro on a limb overhead . . . where the
    buck turns furiously at the hunter,

Where the rattlesnake suns his flabby length on a rock . . . where the
    otter is feeding on fish,
Where the alligator in his tough pimples sleeps by the bayou,
Where the black bear is searching for roots or honey . . . where the
    beaver pats the mud with his paddle-tail;
Over the growing sugar . . . over the cottonplant . . . over the rice in
    its low moist field;
Over the sharp-peaked farmhouse with its scalloped scum and slen-
    der shoots from the gutters;
Over the western persimmon . . . over the longleaved corn and the
    delicate blueflowered flax;
Over the white and brown buckwheat, a hummer and a buzzer there
    with the rest,
Over the dusky green of the rye as it ripples and shades in the breeze;
Scaling mountains . . . pulling myself cautiously up . . . holding on by
    low scragged limbs,
Walking the path worn in the grass and beat through the leaves of the
    brush;
Where the quail is whistling betwixt the woods and the wheatlot,
Where the bat flies in the July eve . . . where the great goldbug drops
    through the dark;
Where the flails keep time on the barn floor,
Where the brook puts out of the roots of the old tree and flows to the
    meadow,
Where cattle stand and shake away flies with the tremulous shudder-
    ing of their hides,
Where the cheese-cloth hangs in the kitchen, and andirons straddle
    the hearth-slab, and cobwebs fall in festoons from the rafters;
Where triphammers crash . . . where the press is whirling its cylinders;
Wherever the human heart beats with terrible throes out of its ribs;
Where the pear-shaped balloon is floating aloft . . . floating in it
    myself and looking composedly down;
Where the life-car is drawn on the slipnoose . . . where the heat
    hatches pale-green eggs in the dented sand,
Where the she-whale swims with her calves and never forsakes them,
Where the steamship trails hindways its long pennant of smoke,
Where the ground-shark's fin cuts like a black chip out of the water,
Where the half-burned brig is riding on unknown currents,
Where shells grow to her slimy deck, and the dead are corrupting
    below;
Where the striped and starred flag is borne at the head of the
    regiments;
Approaching Manhattan, up by the long-stretching island,

Under Niagara, the cataract falling like a veil over my countenance;
Upon a door-step . . . upon the horse-block of hard wood outside,
Upon the race-course, or enjoying pic-nics or jigs or a good game of
    base-ball,
At he-festivals with blackguard jibes and ironical license and bull-
    dances and drinking and laughter,
At the cider-mill, tasting the sweet of the brown sqush . . . sucking the
    juice through a straw,
At apple-pealings, wanting kisses for all the red fruit I find,
At musters and beach-parties and friendly bees and huskings and
    house-raisings;
Where the mockingbird sounds his delicious gurgles, and cackles and
    screams and weeps,
Where the hay-rick stands in the barnyard, and the dry-stalks are scat-
    tered, and the brood cow waits in the hovel,
Where the bull advances to do his masculine work, and the stud to the
    mare, and the cock is treading the hen,
Where the heifers browse, and the geese nip their food with short jerks;
Where the sundown shadows lengthen over the limitless and lone-
    some prairie,
Where the herds of buffalo make a crawling spread of the square miles
    far and near;
Where the hummingbird shimmers . . . where the neck of the
    longlived swan is curving and winding;
Where the laughing-gull scoots by the slappy shore and laughs her
    near-human laugh;
Where beehives range on a gray bench in the garden half-hid by the
    high weeds;
Where the band-necked partridges roost in a ring on the ground with
    their heads out;
Where burial coaches enter the arched gates of a cemetery;
Where winter wolves bark amid wastes of snow and icicled trees;
Where the yellow-crowned heron comes to the edge of the marsh at
    night and feeds upon small crabs;
Where the splash of swimmers and divers cools the warm noon;
Where the katydid works her chromatic reed on the walnut-tree over
    the well;
Through patches of citrons and cucumbers with silver-wired leaves,
Through the salt-lick or orange glade . . . or under conical firs;
Through the gymnasium . . . through the curtained saloon . . . through
    the office or public hall;
Pleased with the native and pleased with the foreign . . . pleased with
    the new and old,

Pleased with women, the homely as well as the handsome,
Pleased with the quakeress as she puts off her bonnet and talks
    melodiously,
Pleased with the primitive tunes of the choir of the whitewashed
    church,
Pleased with the earnest words of the sweating Methodist preacher,
    or any preacher . . . looking seriously at the camp-meeting;
Looking in at the shop-windows in Broadway the whole forenoon . . .
    pressing the flesh of my nose to the thick plate-glass,
Wandering the same afternoon with my face turned up to the clouds;
My right and left arms round the sides of two friends and I in the
    middle;
Coming home with the bearded and dark-cheeked bush-boy . . .
    riding behind him at the drape of the day;
Far from the settlements studying the print of animals' feet, or the
    moccasin print;
By the cot in the hospital reaching lemonade to a feverish patient,
By the coffined corpse when all is still, examining with a candle;
Voyaging to every port to dicker and adventure;
Hurrying with the modern crowd, as eager and fickle as any,
Hot toward one I hate, ready in my madness to knife him;
Solitary at midnight in my back yard, my thoughts gone from me
    a long while,
Walking the old hills of Judea with the beautiful gentle god by my
    side;
Speeding through space . . . speeding through heaven and the stars,
Speeding amid the seven satellites and the broad ring and the diame-
    ter of eighty thousand miles,
Speeding with tailed meteors . . . throwing fire-balls like the rest,
Carrying the crescent child that carries its own full mother in its belly;
Storming enjoying planning loving cautioning,
Backing and filling, appearing and disappearing,
I tread day and night such roads.

I visit the orchards of God and look at the spheric product,
And look at quintillions ripened, and look at quintillions green.

I fly the flight of the fluid and swallowing soul,
My course runs below the soundings of plummets.

I help myself to material and immaterial,
No guard can shut me off, no law can prevent me.

I anchor my ship for a little while only,
My messengers continually cruise away or bring their returns to me.

I go hunting polar furs and the seal . . . leaping chası
    pointed staff . . . clinging to topples of brittle anɪ

I ascend to the foretruck . . . I take my place late at nig
    nest . . . we sail through the arctic sea . . . it is plenɪ
Through the clear atmosphere I stretch around or
    beauty,
The enormous masses of ice pass me and I pass them
    is plain in all directions,
The white-topped mountains point up in the distance .
    my fancies toward them;
We are about approaching some great battlefield in which we are souɪ
    to be engaged,
We pass the colossal outposts of the encampments . . . we pass with
    still feet and caution;
Or we are entering by the suburbs some vast and ruined city . . . the
    blocks and fallen architecture more than all the living cities of
    the globe.

I am a free companion . . . I bivouac by invading watchfires.

I turn the bridegroom out of bed and stay with the bride myself,
And tighten her all night to my thighs and lips.

My voice is the wife's voice, the screech by the rail of the stairs,
They fetch my man's body up dripping and drowned.

I understand the large hearts of heroes,
The courage of present times and all times;
How the skipper saw the crowded and rudderless wreck of the
    steamship, and death chasing it up and down the storm,
How he knuckled tight and gave not back one inch, and was faithful
    of days and faithful of nights,
And chalked in large letters on a board, Be of good cheer, We will not
    desert you;
How he saved the drifting company at last,
How the lank loose-gowned women looked when boated from the
    side of their prepared graves,
How the silent old-faced infants, and the lifted sick, and the sharp-
    lipped unshaved men;
All this I swallow and it tastes good . . . I like it well, and it becomes mine,
I am the man . . . I suffered . . . I was there.

The disdain and calmness of martyrs,
The mother condemned for a witch and burnt with dry wood, and
    her children gazing on;

slave that flags in the race and leans by the fence, blow-
covered with sweat,
that sting like needles his legs and neck,
us buckshot and the bullets,
l or am.

nded slave . . . I wince at the bite of the dogs,
spair are upon me . . . crack and again crack the
nen,
he rails of the fence . . . my gore dribs thinned with the ooze
of my skin,
I fall on the weeds and stones,
The riders spur their unwilling horses and haul close,
They taunt my dizzy ears . . . they beat me violently over the head
with their whip-stocks.

Agonies are one of my changes of garments;
I do not ask the wounded person how he feels . . . I myself become
the wounded person,
My hurt turns livid upon me as I lean on a cane and observe.

I am the mashed fireman with breastbone broken . . . tumbling walls
buried me in their debris,
Heat and smoke I inspired . . . I heard the yelling shouts of my
comrades,
I heard the distant click of their picks and shovels;
They have cleared the beams away . . . they tenderly lift me forth.

I lie in the night air in my red shirt . . . the pervading hush is for my
sake,
Painless after all I lie, exhausted but not so unhappy,
White and beautiful are the faces around me . . . the heads are bared
of their fire-caps,
The kneeling crowd fades with the light of the torches.

Distant and dead resuscitate,
They show as the dial or move as the hands of me . . . and I am the
clock myself.

I am an old artillerist, and tell of some fort's bombardment . . . and am
there again.

Again the reveille of drummers . . . again the attacking cannon and
mortars and howitzers,
Again the attacked send their cannon responsive.

I take part . . . I see and hear the whole,

The cries and curses and roar . . . the plaudits for well aimed shots,
The ambulanza slowly passing and trailing its red drip,
Workmen searching after damages and to make indispensible repairs,
The fall of grenades through the rent roof . . . the fan-shaped explosion,
The whizz of limbs heads stone wood and iron high in the air.

Again gurgles the mouth of my dying general . . . he furiously waves
    with his hand,
He gasps through the clot . . . Mind not me . . . mind . . . the
    entrenchments.

I tell not the fall of Alamo . . . not one escaped to tell the fall of
    Alamo,
The hundred and fifty are dumb yet at Alamo.

Hear now the tale of a jetblack sunrise,
Hear of the murder in cold blood of four hundred and twelve young
    men.

Retreating they had formed in a hollow square with their baggage for
    breastworks,
Nine hundred lives out of the surrounding enemy's nine times their
    number was the price they took in advance,
Their colonel was wounded and their ammunition gone,
They treated for an honorable capitulation, received writing and seal,
    gave up their arms, and marched back prisoners of war.

They were the glory of the race of rangers,
Matchless with a horse, a rifle, a song, a supper or a courtship,
Large, turbulent, brave, handsome, generous, proud and affectionate,
Bearded, sunburnt, dressed in the free costume of hunters,
Not a single one over thirty years of age.

The second Sunday morning they were brought out in squads and
    massacred . . . it was beautiful early summer,
The work commenced about five o'clock and was over by eight.

None obeyed the command to kneel,
Some made a mad and helpless rush . . . some stood stark and straight,
A few fell at once, shot in the temple or heart . . . the living and dead
    lay together,
The maimed and mangled dug in the dirt . . . the new-comers saw
    them there;
Some half-killed attempted to crawl away,
These were dispatched with bayonets or battered with the blunts of
    muskets;

A youth not seventeen years old seized his assassin till two more came
    to release him,
The three were all torn, and covered with the boy's blood.

At eleven o'clock began the burning of the bodies;
And that is the tale of the murder of the four hundred and twelve
    young men,
And that was a jetblack sunrise.

Did you read in the seabooks of the oldfashioned frigate-fight?
Did you learn who won by the light of the moon and stars?

Our foe was no skulk in his ship, I tell you,
His was the English pluck, and there is no tougher or truer, and never
    was, and never will be;
Along the lowered eve he came, horribly raking us.

We closed with him . . . the yards entangled . . . the cannon touched,
My captain lashed fast with his own hands.

We had received some eighteen-pound shots under the water,
On our lower-gun-deck two large pieces had burst at the first fire,
    killing all around and blowing up overhead.

Ten o'clock at night, and the full moon shining and the leaks on the
    gain, and five feet of water reported,
The master-at-arms loosing the prisoners confined in the after-hold
    to give them a chance for themselves.

The transit to and from the magazine was now stopped by the sentinels,
They saw so many strange faces they did not know whom to trust.

Our frigate was afire . . . the other asked if we demanded quarters?
    if our colors were struck and the fighting done?

I laughed content when I heard the voice of my little captain,
We have not struck, he composedly cried, We have just begun our
    part of the fighting.

Only three guns were in use,
One was directed by the captain himself against the enemy's mainmast,
Two well-served with grape and canister silenced his musketry and
    cleared his decks.

The tops alone seconded the fire of this little battery, especially the
    maintop,
They all held out bravely during the whole of the action.

Not a moment's cease,

The leaks gained fast on the pumps . . . the fire eat toward the powder-
    magazine,
One of the pumps was shot away . . . it was generally thought we were
    sinking.

Serene stood the little captain,
He was not hurried . . . his voice was neither high nor low,
His eyes gave more light to us than our battle-lanterns.

Toward twelve at night, there in the beams of the moon they surren-
    dered to us.

Stretched and still lay the midnight,
Two great hulls motionless on the breast of the darkness,
Our vessel riddled and slowly sinking . . . preparations to pass to the
    one we had conquered,
The captain on the quarter deck coldly giving his orders through a
    countenance white as a sheet,
Near by the corpse of the child that served in the cabin,
The dead face of an old salt with long white hair and carefully curled
    whiskers,
The flames spite of all that could be done flickering aloft and below,
The husky voices of the two or three officers yet fit for duty,
Formless stacks of bodies and bodies by themselves . . . dabs of flesh
    upon the masts and spars,
The cut of cordage and dangle of rigging . . . the slight shock of the
    soothe of waves,
Black and impassive guns, and litter of powder-parcels, and the strong
    scent,
Delicate sniffs of the seabreeze . . . smells of sedgy grass and fields by
    the shore . . . death-messages given in charge to survivors,
The hiss of the surgeon's knife and the gnawing teeth of his saw,
The wheeze, the cluck, the swash of falling blood . . . the short wild
    scream, the long dull tapering groan,
These so . . . these irretrievable.

O Christ! My fit is mastering me!
What the rebel said gaily adjusting his throat to the rope-noose,
What the savage at the stump, his eye-sockets empty, his mouth spirt-
    ing whoops and defiance,
What stills the traveler come to the vault at Mount Vernon,
What sobers the Brooklyn boy as he looks down the shores of the
    Wallabout and remembers the prison ships,
What burnt the gums of the redcoat at Saratoga when he surrendered
    his brigades,

These become mine and me every one, and they are but little,
I become as much more as I like.

I become any presence or truth of humanity here,
And see myself in prison shaped like another man,
And feel the dull unintermitted pain.

For me the keepers of convicts shoulder their carbines and keep
watch,
It is I let out in the morning and barred at night.

Not a mutineer walks handcuffed to the jail, but I am handcuffed to
him and walk by his side,
I am less the jolly one there, and more the silent one with sweat on
my twitching lips.

Not a youngster is taken for larceny, but I go up too and am tried and
sentenced.

Not a cholera patient lies at the last gasp, but I also lie at the last gasp,
My face is ash-colored, my sinews gnarl . . . away from me people
retreat.

Askers embody themselves in me, and I am embodied in them,
I project my hat and sit shamefaced and beg.

I rise extatic through all, and sweep with the true gravitation,
The whirling and whirling is elemental within me.

Somehow I have been stunned. Stand back!
Give me a little time beyond my cuffed head and slumbers and dreams
and gaping,
I discover myself on a verge of the usual mistake.

That I could forget the mockers and insults!
That I could forget the trickling tears and the blows of the bludgeons
and hammers!
That I could look with a separate look on my own crucifixion and
bloody crowning!

I remember . . . I resume the overstaid fraction,
The grave of rock multiplies what has been confided to it . . . or to
any graves,
The corpses rise . . . the gashes heal . . . the fastenings roll away.

I troop forth replenished with supreme power, one of an average
unending procession,
We walk the roads of Ohio and Massachusetts and Virginia and

Wisconsin and New York and New Orleans and Texas and
Montreal and San Francisco and Charleston and Savannah and
Mexico,
Inland and by the seacoast and boundary lines . . . and we pass the
boundary lines.

Our swift ordinances are on their way over the whole earth,
The blossoms we wear in our hats are the growth of two thousand
years.

Eleves I salute you,
I see the approach of your numberless gangs . . . I see you understand
yourselves and me,
And know that they who have eyes are divine, and the blind and lame
are equally divine,
And that my steps drag behind yours yet go before them,
And are aware how I am with you no more than I am with
everybody.

The friendly and flowing savage . . . Who is he?
Is he waiting for civilization or past it and mastering it?

Is he some southwesterner raised outdoors? Is he Canadian?
Is he from the Mississippi country? or from Iowa, Oregon or
California? or from the mountains? or prairie life or bush-life?
or from the sea?

Wherever he goes men and women accept and desire him,
They desire he should like them and touch them and speak to them
and stay with them.

Behaviour lawless as snow-flakes . . . words simple as grass . . .
uncombed head and laughter and naivete;
Slowstepping feet and the common features, and the common modes
and emanations,
They descend in new forms from the tips of his fingers,
They are wafted with the odor of his body or breath . . . they fly out
of the glance of his eyes.

Flaunt of the sunshine I need not your bask . . . lie over,
You light surfaces only . . . I force the surfaces and the depths also.

Earth! you seem to look for something at my hands,
Say old topknot! what do you want?

Man or woman! I might tell how I like you, but cannot,
And might tell what it is in me and what it is in you, but cannot,

And might tell the pinings I have . . . the pulse of my nights and days.

Behold I do not give lectures or a little charity,
What I give I give out of myself.

You there, impotent, loose in the knees, open your scarfed chops till
    I blow grit within you,
Spread your palms and lift the flaps of your pockets,
I am not to be denied . . . I compel . . . I have stores plenty and to
    spare,
And any thing I have I bestow.

I do not ask who you are . . . that is not important to me,
You can do nothing and be nothing but what I will infold you.

To a drudge of the cottonfields or emptier of privies I lean . . . on his
    right cheek I put the family kiss,
And in my soul I swear I never will deny him.

On women fit for conception I start bigger and nimbler babes,
This day I am jetting the stuff of far more arrogant republics.

To any one dying . . . thither I speed and twist the knob of the door,
Turn the bedclothes toward the foot of the bed,
Let the physician and the priest go home.

I seize the descending man . . . I raise him with resistless will.

O despairer, here is my neck,
By God! you shall not go down! Hang your whole weight upon me.

I dilate you with tremendous breath . . . I buoy you up;
Every room of the house do I fill with an armed force . . . lovers of
    me, bafflers of graves:
Sleep! I and they keep guard all night;
Not doubt, not decease shall dare to lay finger upon you,
I have embraced you, and henceforth possess you to myself,
And when you rise in the morning you will find what I tell you
    is so.

I am he bringing help for the sick as they pant on their backs,
And for strong upright men I bring yet more needed help.

I heard what was said of the universe,
Heard it and heard of several thousand years;
It is middling well as far as it goes . . . but is that all?

Magnifying and applying come I,
Outbidding at the start the old cautious hucksters,

The most they offer for mankind and eternity less than a spirt of my
    own seminal wet,
Taking myself the exact dimensions of Jehovah and laying them away,
Lithographing Kronos and Zeus his son, and Hercules his grandson,
Buying drafts of Osiris and Isis and Belus and Brahma and Adonai,
In my portfolio placing Manito loose, and Allah on a leaf, and the
    crucifix engraved,
With Odin, and the hideous-faced Mexitli, and all idols and images,
Honestly taking them all for what they are worth, and not a cent
    more,
Admitting they were alive and did the work of their day,
Admitting they bore mites as for unfledged birds who have now to
    rise and fly and sing for themselves,
Accepting the rough deific sketches to fill out better in myself . . .
    bestowing them freely on each man and woman I see,
Discovering as much or more in a framer framing a house,
Putting higher claims for him there with his rolled-up sleeves, driving
    the mallet and chisel;
Not objecting to special revelations . . . considering a curl of smoke or
    a hair on the back of my hand as curious as any revelation;
Those ahold of fire-engines and hook-and-ladder ropes more to me
    than the gods of the antique wars,
Minding their voices peal through the crash of destruction,
Their brawny limbs passing safe over charred laths . . . their white fore-
    heads whole and unhurt out of the flames;
By the mechanic's wife with her babe at her nipple interceding for
    every person born;
Three scythes at harvest whizzing in a row from three lusty angels
    with shirts bagged out at their waists;
The snag-toothed hostler with red hair redeeming sins past and to
    come,
Selling all he possesses and traveling on foot to fee lawyers for his
    brother and sit by him while he is tried for forgery:
What was strewn in the amplest strewing the square rod about me, and
    not filling the square rod then;
The bull and the bug never worshipped half enough,
Dung and dirt more admirable than was dreamed,
The supernatural of no account . . . myself waiting my time to be one
    of the supremes,
The day getting ready for me when I shall do as much good as the
    best, and be as prodigious,
Guessing when I am it will not tickle me much to receive puffs out
    of pulpit or print;

By my life-lumps! becoming already a creator!
Putting myself here and now to the ambushed womb of the shadows!

. . . A call in the midst of the crowd,
My own voice, orotund sweeping and final.

Come my children,
Come my boys and girls, and my women and household and
    intimates,
Now the performer launches his nerve . . . he has passed his prelude
    on the reeds within.

Easily written loosefingered chords! I feel the thrum of their climax
    and close.

My head evolves on my neck,
Music rolls, but not from the organ . . . folks are around me, but they
    are no household of mine.

Ever the hard and unsunk ground,
Ever the eaters and drinkers . . . ever the upward and downward sun
    . . . ever the air and the ceaseless tides,
Ever myself and my neighbors, refreshing and wicked and real,
Ever the old inexplicable query . . . ever that thorned thumb—that
    breath of itches and thirsts,
Ever the vexer's hoot! hoot! till we find where the sly one hides and
    bring him forth;
Ever love . . . ever the sobbing liquid of life,
Ever the bandage under the chin . . . ever the tressels of death.

Here and there with dimes on the eyes walking,
To feed the greed of the belly the brains liberally spooning,
Tickets buying or taking or selling, but in to the feast never once
    going;
Many sweating and ploughing and thrashing, and then the chaff for
    payment receiving,
A few idly owning, and they the wheat continually claiming.

This is the city . . . and I am one of the citizens;
Whatever interests the rest interests me . . . politics, churches, news-
    papers, schools,
Benevolent societies, improvements, banks, tariffs, steamships, facto-
    ries, markets,
Stocks and stores and real estate and personal estate.

They who piddle and patter here in collars and tailed coats . . . I am
    aware who they are . . . and that they are not worms or fleas,

I acknowledge the duplicates of myself under all the scrape-lipped and
     pipe-legged concealments.

The weakest and shallowest is deathless with me,
What I do and say the same waits for them,
Every thought that flounders in me the same flounders in them.

I know perfectly well my own egotism,
And know my omniverous words, and cannot say any less,
And would fetch you whoever you are flush with myself.

My words are words of a questioning, and to indicate reality;
This printed and bound book . . . but the printer and the printing-
     office boy?
The marriage estate and settlement . . . but the body and mind of the
     bridegroom? also those of the bride?
The panorama of the sea . . . but the sea itself?
The well-taken photographs . . . but your wife or friend close and solid
     in your arms?
The fleet of ships of the line and all the modern improvements . . . but
     the craft and pluck of the admiral?
The dishes and fare and furniture . . . but the host and hostess, and the
     look out of their eyes?
The sky up there . . . yet here or next door or across the way?
The saints and sages in history . . . but you yourself?
Sermons and creeds and theology . . . but the human brain, and
     what is called reason, and what is called love, and what is called
     life?

I do not despise you priests;
My faith is the greatest of faiths and the least of faiths,
Enclosing all worship ancient and modern, and all between ancient
     and modern,
Believing I shall come again upon the earth after five thousand years,
Waiting responses from oracles . . . honoring the gods . . . saluting the
     sun,
Making a fetish of the first rock or stump . . . powowing with sticks
     in the circle of obis,
Helping the lama or brahmin as he trims the lamps of the idols,
Dancing yet through the streets in a phallic procession . . . rapt and
     austere in the woods, a gymnosophist,
Drinking mead from the skull-cup . . . to shasta and vedas admirant . . .
     minding the koran,
Walking the teokallis, spotted with gore from the stone and knife—
     beating the serpent-skin drum;

Accepting the gospels, accepting him that was crucified, knowing
    assuredly that he is divine,
To the mass kneeling—to the puritan's prayer rising—sitting patiently
    in a pew,
Ranting and frothing in my insane crisis—waiting dead-like till my
    spirit arouses me;
Looking forth on pavement and land, and outside of pavement and
    land,
Belonging to the winders of the circuit of circuits.

One of that centripetal and centrifugal gang,
I turn and talk like a man leaving charges before a journey.

Down-hearted doubters, dull and excluded,
Frivolous sullen moping angry affected disheartened atheistical,
I know every one of you, and know the unspoken interrogatories,
By experience I know them.

How the flukes splash!
How they contort rapid as lightning, with spasms and spouts of blood!

Be at peace bloody flukes of doubters and sullen mopers,
I take my place among you as much as among any;
The past is the push of you and me and all precisely the same,
And the day and night are for you and me and all,
And what is yet untried and afterward is for you and me and all.

I do not know what is untried and afterward,
But I know it is sure and alive and sufficient.

Each who passes is considered, and each who stops is considered, and
    not a single one can it fail.

It cannot fail the young man who died and was buried,
Nor the young woman who died and was put by his side,
Nor the little child that peeped in at the door and then drew back and
    was never seen again,
Nor the old man who has lived without purpose, and feels it with bit-
    terness worse than gall,
Nor him in the poorhouse tubercled by rum and the bad disorder,
Nor the numberless slaughtered and wrecked . . . nor the brutish
    koboo, called the ordure of humanity,
Nor the sacs merely floating with open mouths for food to slip in,
Nor any thing in the earth, or down in the oldest graves of the earth,
Nor any thing in the myriads of spheres, nor one of the myriads of
    myriads that inhabit them,

Nor the present, nor the least wisp that is known.

It is time to explain myself . . . let us stand up.

What is known I strip away . . . I launch all men and women forward
    with me into the unknown.

The clock indicates the moment . . . but what does eternity indicate?

Eternity lies in bottomless reservoirs . . . its buckets are rising forever
    and ever,
They pour and they pour and they exhale away.

We have thus far exhausted trillions of winters and summers;
There are trillions ahead, and trillions ahead of them.

Births have brought us richness and variety,
And other births will bring us richness and variety.

I do not call one greater and one smaller,
That which fills its period and place is equal to any.

Were mankind murderous or jealous upon you my brother or my
    sister?
I am sorry for you . . . they are not murderous or jealous upon me;
All has been gentle with me . . . I keep no account with lamentation;
What have I to do with lamentation?

I am an acme of things accomplished, and I an encloser of things to
    be.

My feet strike an apex of the apices of the stairs,
On every step bunches of ages, and larger bunches between the steps,
All below duly traveled—and still I mount and mount.

Rise after rise bow the phantoms behind me,
Afar down I see the huge first Nothing, the vapor from the nostrils of
    death,
I know I was even there . . . I waited unseen and always,
And slept while God carried me through the lethargic mist,
And took my time . . . and took no hurt from the fœtid carbon.

Long I was hugged close . . . long and long.

Immense have been the preparations for me,
Faithful and friendly the arms that have helped me.

Cycles ferried my cradle, rowing and rowing like cheerful boatmen;
For room to me stars kept aside in their own rings,
They sent influences to look after what was to hold me.

Before I was born out of my mother generations guided me,
My embryo has never been torpid ... nothing could overlay it;
For it the nebula cohered to an orb ... the long slow strata piled to
    rest it on ... vast vegetables gave it sustenance,
Monstrous sauroids transported it in their mouths and deposited it
    with care.

All forces have been steadily employed to complete and delight me,
Now I stand on this spot with my soul.

Span of youth! Ever-pushed elasticity! Manhood balanced and florid
    and full!

My lovers suffocate me!
Crowding my lips, and thick in the pores of my skin,
Jostling me through streets and public halls ... coming naked to me
    at night,
Crying by day Ahoy from the rocks of the river ... swinging and
    chirping over my head,
Calling my name from flowerbeds or vines or tangled underbrush,
Or while I swim in the bath ... or drink from the pump at the
    corner ... or the curtain is down at the opera ... or I glimpse at
    a woman's face in the railroad car;
Lighting on every moment of my life,
Bussing my body with soft and balsamic busses,
Noiselessly passing handfuls out of their hearts and giving them to be
    mine.

Old age superbly rising! Ineffable grace of dying days!

Every condition promulges not only itself ... it promulges what grows
    after and out of itself,
And the dark hush promulges as much as any.

I open my scuttle at night and see the far-sprinkled systems,
And all I see, multiplied as high as I can cipher, edge but the rim of
    the farther systems.

Wider and wider they spread, expanding and always expanding,
Outward and outward and forever outward.

My sun has his sun, and round him obediently wheels,
He joins with his partners a group of superior circuit,
And greater sets follow, making specks of the greatest inside them.

There is no stoppage, and never can be stoppage;
If I and you and the worlds and all beneath or upon their surfaces, and

all the palpable life, were this moment reduced back to a pallid
float, it would not avail in the long run,
We should surely bring up again where we now stand,
And as surely go as much farther, and then farther and farther.

A few quadrillions of eras, a few octillions of cubic leagues, do not
hazard the span, or make it impatient,
They are but parts . . . any thing is but a part.

See ever so far . . . there is limitless space outside of that,
Count ever so much . . . there is limitless time around that.

Our rendezvous is fitly appointed . . . God will be there and wait till
we come.

I know I have the best of time and space—and that I was never mea-
sured, and never will be measured.

I tramp a perpetual journey,
My signs are a rain-proof coat and good shoes and a staff cut from the
woods;
No friend of mine takes his ease in my chair,
I have no chair, nor church nor philosophy;
I lead no man to a dinner-table or library or exchange,
But each man and each woman of you I lead upon a knoll,
My left hand hooks you round the waist,
My right hand points to landscapes of continents, and a plain public
road.

Not I, not any one else can travel that road for you,
You must travel it for yourself.

It is not far . . . it is within reach,
Perhaps you have been on it since you were born, and did not
know,
Perhaps it is every where on water and on land.

Shoulder your duds, and I will mine, and let us hasten forth;
Wonderful cities and free nations we shall fetch as we go.

If you tire, give me both burdens, and rest the chuff of your hand on
my hip,
And in due time you shall repay the same service to me;
For after we start we never lie by again.

This day before dawn I ascended a hill and looked at the crowded
heaven,
And I said to my spirit, When we become the enfolders of those orbs

and the pleasure and knowledge of every thing in them, shall we
be filled and satisfied then?
And my spirit said No, we level that lift to pass and continue
beyond.

You are also asking me questions, and I hear you;
I answer that I cannot answer . . . you must find out for yourself.

Sit awhile wayfarer,
Here are biscuits to eat and here is milk to drink,
But as soon as you sleep and renew yourself in sweet clothes I will
certainly kiss you with my goodbye kiss and open the gate for
your egress hence.

Long enough have you dreamed contemptible dreams,
Now I wash the gum from your eyes,
You must habit yourself to the dazzle of the light and of every
moment of your life

Long have you timidly waded, holding a plank by the shore,
Now I will you to be a bold swimmer,
To jump off in the midst of the sea, and rise again and nod to me and
shout, and laughingly dash with your hair.

I am the teacher of athletes,
He that by me spreads a wider breast than my own proves the width
of my own,
He most honors my style who learns under it to destroy the
teacher.

The boy I love, the same becomes a man not through derived power
but in his own right,
Wicked, rather than virtuous out of conformity or fear,
Fond of his sweetheart, relishing well his steak,
Unrequited love or a slight cutting him worse than a wound cuts,
First rate to ride, to fight, to hit the bull's eye, to sail a skiff, to sing
a song or play on the banjo,
Preferring scars and faces pitted with smallpox over all latherers and
those that keep out of the sun.

I teach straying from me, yet who can stray from me?
I follow you whoever you are from the present hour;
My words itch at your ears till you understand them.

I do not say these things for a dollar, or to fill up the time while I wait
for a boat;
It is you talking just as much as myself . . . I act as the tongue of you,

It was tied in your mouth . . . in mine it begins to be loosened.

I swear I will never mention love or death inside a house,
And I swear I never will translate myself at all, only to him or her who
    privately stays with me in the open air.

If you would understand me go to the heights or water-shore,
The nearest gnat is an explanation and a drop or the motion of waves
    a key,
The maul the oar and the handsaw second my words.

No shuttered room or school can commune with me,
But roughs and little children better than they.

The young mechanic is closest to me . . . he knows me pretty well,
The woodman that takes his axe and jug with him shall take me with
    him all day,
The farmboy ploughing in the field feels good at the sound of my
    voice,
In vessels that sail my words must sail . . . I go with fishermen and sea-
    men, and love them,
My face rubs to the hunter's face when he lies down alone in his
    blanket,
The driver thinking of me does not mind the jolt of his wagon,
The young mother and old mother shall comprehend me,
The girl and the wife rest the needle a moment and forget where they
    are,
They and all would resume what I have told them.

I have said that the soul is not more than the body,
And I have said that the body is not more than the soul,
And nothing, not God, is greater to one than one's-self is,
And whoever walks a furlong without sympathy walks to his own
    funeral, dressed in his shroud,
And I or you pocketless of a dime may purchase the pick of the earth,
And to glance with an eye or show a bean in its pod confounds the
    learning of all times,
And there is no trade or employment but the young man following it
    may become a hero,
And there is no object so soft but it makes a hub for the wheeled
    universe,
And any man or woman shall stand cool and supercilious before a
    million universes.

And I call to mankind, Be not curious about God,
For I who am curious about each am not curious about God,

No array of terms can say how much I am at peace about God and
   about death.

I hear and behold God in every object, yet I understand God not in
   the least,
Nor do I understand who there can be more wonderful than myself.

Why should I wish to see God better than this day?
I see something of God each hour of the twenty-four, and each
   moment then,
In the faces of men and women I see God, and in my own face in the
   glass;
I find letters from God dropped in the street, and every one is signed
   by God's name,
And I leave them where they are, for I know that others will punctu-
   ally come forever and ever.

And as to you death, and you bitter hug of mortality . . . it is idle to
   try to alarm me.

To his work without flinching the accoucheur comes,
I see the elderhand pressing receiving supporting,
I recline by the sills of the exquisite flexible doors . . . and mark the
   outlet, and mark the relief and escape.

And as to you corpse I think you are good manure, but that does not
   offend me,
I smell the white roses sweetscented and growing,
I reach to the leafy lips . . . I reach to the polished breasts of melons.

And as to you life, I reckon you are the leavings of many deaths,
No doubt I have died myself ten thousand times before.

I hear you whispering there O stars of heaven,
O suns . . . O grass of graves . . . O perpetual transfers and promotions
   . . . if you do not say anything how can I say anything?

Of the turbid pool that lies in the autumn forest,
Of the moon that descends the steeps of the soughing twilight,
Toss, sparkles of day and dusk . . . toss on the black stems that decay in
   the muck,
Toss to the moaning gibberish of the dry limbs.

I ascend from the moon . . . I ascend from the night,
And perceive of the ghastly glitter the sunbeams reflected,
And debouch to the steady and central from the offspring great or
   small.

There is that in me . . . I do not know what it is . . . but I know it is
in me.

Wrenched and sweaty . . . calm and cool then my body becomes;
I sleep . . . I sleep long.

I do not know it . . . it is without name . . . it is a word unsaid,
It is not in any dictionary or utterance or symbol.

Something it swings on more than the earth I swing on,
To it the creation is the friend whose embracing awakes me.

Perhaps I might tell more . . . Outlines! I plead for my brothers and
sisters.

Do you see O my brothers and sisters?
It is not chaos or death . . . it is form and union and plan . . . it is eter-
nal life . . . it is happiness.

The past and present wilt . . . I have filled them and emptied them,
And proceed to fill my next fold of the future.

Listener up there! Here you . . . what have you to confide to me?
Look in my face while I snuff the sidle of evening,
Talk honestly, for no one else hears you, and I stay only a minute
longer.

Do I contradict myself?
Very well then . . . I contradict myself;
I am large . . . I contain multitudes.

I concentrate toward them that are nigh . . . I wait on the door-slab.

Who has done his day's work and will soonest be through with his
supper?
Who wishes to walk with me?

Will you speak before I am gone? Will you prove already too late?

The spotted hawk swoops by and accuses me . . . he complains of my
gab and my loitering.

I too am not a bit tamed . . . I too am untranslatable,
I sound my barbaric yawp over the roofs of the world.

The last scud of day holds back for me,
It flings my likeness after the rest and true as any on the shadowed
wilds,
It coaxes me to the vapor and the dusk.

I depart as air . . . I shake my white locks at the runaway sun,
I effuse my flesh in eddies and drift it in lacy jags.

I bequeath myself to the dirt to grow from the grass I love,
If you want me again look for me under your bootsoles.

You will hardly know who I am or what I mean,
But I shall be good health to you nevertheless,
And filter and fibre your blood.

Failing to fetch me at first keep encouraged,
Missing me one place search another,
I stop some where waiting for you

LEAVES OF GRASS

COME closer to me,
    Push close my lovers and take the best I possess,
Yield closer and closer and give me the best you possess.

This is unfinished business with me . . . how is it with you?
I was chilled with the cold types and cylinder and wet paper between
    us.

I pass so poorly with paper and types . . . I must pass with the contact
    of bodies and souls.

I do not thank you for liking me as I am, and liking the touch of me
    . . . I know that it is good for you to do so.

Were all educations practical and ornamental well displayed out of
    me, what would it amount to?
Were I as the head teacher or charitable proprietor or wise statesman,
    what would it amount to?
Were I to you as the boss employing and paying you, would that sat-
    isfy you?

The learned and virtuous and benevolent, and the usual terms;
A man like me, and never the usual terms.

Neither a servant nor a master am I,
I take no sooner a large price than a small price . . . I will have my
    own whoever enjoys me,
I will be even with you, and you shall be even with me.

If you are a workman or workwoman I stand as nigh as the nighest
    that works in the same shop,
If you bestow gifts on your brother or dearest friend, I demand as
    good as your brother or dearest friend,
If your lover or husband or wife is welcome by day or night, I must
    be personally as welcome;

If you have become degraded or ill, then I will become so for your
sake;
If you remember your foolish and outlawed deeds, do you think I
cannot remember my foolish and outlawed deeds?
If you carouse at the table I say I will carouse at the opposite side of
the table;
If you meet some stranger in the street and love him or her, do I not
often meet strangers in the street and love them?
If you see a good deal remarkable in me I see just as much remark-
able in you.

Why what have you thought of yourself?
Is it you then that thought yourself less?
Is it you that thought the President greater than you? or the rich bet-
ter off than you? or the educated wiser than you?

Because you are greasy or pimpled—or that you was once drunk, or
a thief, or diseased, or rheumatic, or a prostitute—or are so
now—or from frivolity or impotence—or that you are no
scholar, and never saw your name in print ... do you give in that
you are any less immortal?

Souls of men and women! it is not you I call unseen, unheard,
untouchable and untouching;
It is not you I go argue pro and con about, and to settle whether you
are alive or no;
I own publicly who you are, if nobody else owns ... and see and hear
you, and what you give and take;
What is there you cannot give and take?

I see not merely that you are polite or whitefaced ... married or
single ... citizens of old states or citizens of new states ...
eminent in some profession ... a lady or gentleman in a parlor
... or dressed in the jail uniform ... or pulpit uniform,
Not only the free Utahan, Kansian, or Arkansian ... not only the free
Cuban ... not merely the slave ... not Mexican native, or
Flatfoot, or negro from Africa,
Iroquois eating the warflesh—fishtearer in his lair of rocks and sand
... Esquimaux in the dark cold snowhouse ... Chinese with his
transverse eyes ... Bedowee—or wandering nomad—or taboun-
schik at the head of his droves,
Grown, half-grown, and babe—of this country and every country, in-
doors and outdoors I see ... and all else is behind or through
them.

The wife—and she is not one jot less than the husband,
The daughter—and she is just as good as the son,
The mother—and she is every bit as much as the father.

Offspring of those not rich—boys apprenticed to trades,
Young fellows working on farms and old fellows working on farms;
The naive . . . the simple and hardy . . . he going to the polls to vote
      . . . he who has a good time, and he who has a bad time;
Mechanics, southerners, new arrivals, sailors, mano'warsmen, mer-
      chantmen, coasters,
All these I see . . . but nigher and farther the same I see;
None shall escape me, and none shall wish to escape me.

I bring what you much need, yet always have,
I bring not money or amours or dress or eating . . . but I bring as good;
And send no agent or medium . . . and offer no representative of
      value—but offer the value itself.

There is something that comes home to one now and perpetually,
It is not what is printed or preached or discussed . . . it eludes discus-
      sion and print,
It is not to be put in a book . . . it is not in this book,
It is for you whoever you are . . . it is no farther from you than your
      hearing and sight are from you,
It is hinted by nearest and commonest and readiest . . . it is not them,
      though it is endlessly provoked by them . . . What is there ready
      and near you now?

You may read in many languages and read nothing about it;
You may read the President's message and read nothing about it there,
Nothing in the reports from the state department or treasury depart-
      ment . . . or in the daily papers, or the weekly papers,
Or in the census returns or assessors' returns or prices current or any
      accounts of stock.

The sun and stars that float in the open air . . . the appleshaped earth
      and we upon it . . . surely the drift of them is something grand;
I do not know what it is except that it is grand, and that it is
      happiness,
And that the enclosing purport of us here is not a speculation, or bon-
      mot or reconnoissance,
And that it is not something which by luck may turn out well for us,
      and without luck must be a failure for us,
And not something which may yet be retracted in a certain
      contingency.

The light and shade—the curious sense of body and identity—the
greed that with perfect complaisance devours all things—the
endless pride and outstretching of man—unspeakable joys and
sorrows,
The wonder every one sees in every one else he sees . . . and the won-
ders that fill each minute of time forever and each acre of sur-
face and space forever,
Have you reckoned them as mainly for a trade or farmwork? or for
the profits of a store? or to achieve yourself a position? or to fill
a gentleman's leisure or a lady's leisure?

Have you reckoned the landscape took substance and form that it
might be painted in a picture?
Or men and women that they might be written of, and songs sung?
Or the attraction of gravity and the great laws and harmonious com-
binations and the fluids of the air as subjects for the savans?
Or the brown land and the blue sea for maps and charts?
Or the stars to be put in constellations and named fancy names?
Or that the growth of seeds is for agricultural tables or agriculture
itself?

Old institutions . . . these arts libraries legends collections—and the prac-
tice handed along in manufactures . . . will we rate them so high?
Will we rate our prudence and business so high? . . . I have no objec-
tion,
I rate them as high as the highest . . . but a child born of a woman and
man I rate beyond all rate.

We thought our Union grand and our Constitution grand;
I do not say they are not grand and good—for they are,
I am this day just as much in love with them as you,
But I am eternally in love with you and with all my fellows upon the
earth.

We consider the bibles and religions divine . . . I do not say they are
not divine,
I say they have all grown out of you and may grow out of you still,
It is not they who give the life . . . it is you who give the life;
Leaves are not more shed from the trees or trees from the earth than
they are shed out of you.

The sum of all known value and respect I add up in you whoever you
are;
The President is up there in the White House for you . . . it is not you
who are here for him,

The Secretaries act in their bureaus for you . . . not you here for them,
The Congress convenes every December for you,
Laws, courts, the forming of states, the charters of cities, the going and
coming of commerce and mails are all for you.

All doctrines, all politics and civilization exurge from you,
All sculpture and monuments and anything inscribed anywhere are
tallied in you,
The gist of histories and statistics as far back as the records reach is in
you this hour—and myths and tales the same;
If you were not breathing and walking here where would they all be?
The most renowned poems would be ashes . . . orations and plays
would be vacuums.

All architecture is what you do to it when you look upon it;
Did you think it was in the white or gray stone? or the lines of the
arches and cornices?

All music is what awakens from you when you are reminded by the
instruments,
It is not the violins and the cornets . . . it is not the oboe nor the beat-
ing drums—nor the notes of the baritone singer singing his
sweet romanza . . . nor those of the men's chorus, nor those of
the women's chorus,
It is nearer and farther than they.

Will the whole come back then?
Can each see the signs of the best by a look in the lookingglass? Is
there nothing greater or more?
Does all sit there with you and here with me?

The old forever new things . . . you foolish child! . . . the closest sim-
plest things—this moment with you,
Your person and every particle that relates to your person,
The pulses of your brain waiting their chance and encouragement at
every deed or sight;
Anything you do in public by day, and anything you do in secret
betweendays,
What is called right and what is called wrong . . . what you behold or
touch . . . what causes your anger or wonder,
The anklechain of the slave, the bed of the bedhouse, the cards of the
gambler, the plates of the forger;
What is seen or learned in the street, or intuitively learned,
What is learned in the public school—spelling, reading, writing and
ciphering . . . the blackboard and the teacher's diagrams:

The panes of the windows and all that appears through them . . . the
    going forth in the morning and the aimless spending of the day;
(What is it that you made money? what is it that you got what you
    wanted?)
The usual routine . . . the workshop, factory, yard, office, store,
    or desk;
The jaunt of hunting or fishing, or the life of hunting or fishing,
Pasturelife, foddering, milking and herding, and all the personnel and
    usages;
The plum-orchard and apple-orchard . . . gardening . . . seedlings, cut-
    tings, flowers and vines,
Grains and manures . . . marl, clay, loam . . . the subsoil plough . . . the
    shovel and pick and rake and hoe . . . irrigation and draining;
The currycomb . . . the horse-cloth . . . the halter and bridle and bits
    . . . the very wisps of straw,
The barn and barn-yard . . . the bins and mangers . . . the mows and
    racks:
Manufactures . . . commerce . . . engineering . . . the building of cities,
    and every trade carried on there . . . and the implements of every
    trade,
The anvil and tongs and hammer . . . the axe and wedge . . . the square
    and mitre and jointer and smoothingplane;
The plumbob and trowel and level . . . the wall-scaffold, and the work
    of walls and ceilings . . . or any mason-work:
The ship's compass . . . the sailor's tarpaulin . . . the stays and lanyards,
    and the ground-tackle for anchoring or mooring,
The sloop's tiller . . . the pilot's wheel and bell . . . the yacht or fish-
    smack . . . the great gay-pennanted three-hundred-foot steam-
    boat under full headway, with her proud fat breasts and her
    delicate swift-flashing paddles;
The trail and line and hooks and sinkers . . . the seine, and hauling the
    seine;
Smallarms and rifles . . . the powder and shot and caps and wadding
    . . . the ordnance for war . . . the carriages:
Everyday objects . . . the housechairs, the carpet, the bed and the
    counterpane of the bed, and him or her sleeping at night, and the
    wind blowing, and the indefinite noises:
The snowstorm or rainstorm . . . the tow-trowsers . . . the lodge-hut
    in the woods, and the still-hunt:
City and country . . . fireplace and candle . . . gaslight and heater and
    aqueduct;
The message of the governor, mayor, or chief of police . . . the dishes
    of breakfast or dinner or supper;

The bunkroom, the fire-engine, the string-team, and the car or truck behind;

The paper I write on or you write on . . . and every word we write . . . and every cross and twirl of the pen . . . and the curious way we write what we think . . . yet very faintly;

The directory, the detector, the ledger . . . the books in ranks or the bookshelves . . . the clock attached to the wall,

The ring on your finger . . . the lady's wristlet . . . the hammers of stonebreakers or coppersmiths . . . the druggist's vials and jars;

The etui of surgical instruments, and the etui of oculist's or aurist's instruments, or dentist's instruments;

Glassblowing, grinding of wheat and corn . . . casting, and what is cast . . . tinroofing, shingledressing,

Shipcarpentering, flagging of sidewalks by flaggers . . . dockbuilding, fishcuring, ferrying;

The pump, the piledriver, the great derrick . . . the coalkiln and brick-kiln,

Ironworks or whiteleadworks . . . the sugarhouse . . . steam-saws, and the great mills and factories;

The cottonbale . . . the stevedore's hook . . . the saw and buck of the sawyer . . . the screen of the coalscreener . . . the mould of the moulder . . . the workingknife of the butcher;

The cylinder press . . . the handpress . . . the frisket and tympan . . . the compositor's stick and rule,

The implements for daguerreotyping . . . the tools of the rigger or grappler or sailmaker or blockmaker,

Goods of guttapercha or papiermache . . . colors and brushes . . . glaziers' implements,

The veneer and gluepot . . . the confectioner's ornaments . . . the decanter and glasses . . . the shears and flatiron;

The awl and kneestrap . . . the pint measure and quart measure . . . the counter and stool . . . the writingpen of quill or metal;

Billiards and tenpins . . . the ladders and hanging ropes of the gymnasium, and the manly exercises;

The designs for wallpapers or oilcloths or carpets . . . the fancies for goods for women . . . the bookbinder's stamps;

Leatherdressing, coachmaking, boilermaking, ropetwisting, distilling, signpainting, limeburning, coopering, cottonpicking,

The walkingbeam of the steam-engine . . . the throttle and governors, and the up and down rods,

Stavemachines and plainingmachines . . . the cart of the carman . . . the omnibus . . . the ponderous dray;

The snowplough and two engines pushing it . . . the ride in the

express train of only one car . . . the swift go through a howling
storm:

The bearhunt or coonhunt . . . the bonfire of shavings in the open lot
in the city . . . the crowd of children watching;

The blows of the fighting-man . . . the upper cut and one–two–three;

The shopwindows . . . the coffins in the sexton's wareroom . . . the fruit
on the fruitstand . . . the beef on the butcher's stall,

The bread and cakes in the bakery . . . the white and red pork in the
pork-store;

The milliner's ribbons . . . the dressmaker's patterns . . . the tea-table
. . . the homemade sweetmeats:

The column of wants in the one-cent paper . . . the news by telegraph
. . . the amusements and operas and shows:

The cotton and woolen and linen you wear . . . the money you make
and spend;

Your room and bedroom . . . your piano-forte . . . the stove and
cookpans,

The house you live in . . . the rent . . . the other tenants . . . the
deposite in the savings-bank . . . the trade at the grocery,

The pay on Saturday night . . . the going home, and the purchases;

In them the heft of the heaviest . . . in them far more than you esti-
mated, and far less also,

In them, not yourself . . . you and your soul enclose all things, regard-
less of estimation,

In them your themes and hints and provokers . . . if not, the whole
earth has no themes or hints or provokers, and never had.

I do not affirm what you see beyond is futile . . . I do not advise you
to stop,

I do not say leadings you thought great are not great,

But I say that none lead to greater or sadder or happier than those lead
to.

Will you seek afar off? You surely come back at last,

In things best known to you finding the best or as good as the best,

In folks nearest to you finding also the sweetest and strongest and
lovingest,

Happiness not in another place, but this place . . . not for another hour,
but this hour,

Man in the first you see or touch . . . always in your friend or brother
or nighest neighbor . . . Woman in your mother or lover or wife,

And all else thus far known giving place to men and women.

When the psalm sings instead of the singer,

When the script preaches instead of the preacher,

When the pulpit descends and goes instead of the carver that carved
the supporting desk,

When the sacred vessels or the bits of the eucharist, or the lath and
plast, procreate as effectually as the young silversmiths or bakers,
or the masons in their overalls,

When a university course convinces like a slumbering woman and
child convince,

When the minted gold in the vault smiles like the nightwatchman's
daughter,

When warrantee deeds loafe in chairs opposite and are my friendly
companions,

I intend to reach them my hand and make as much of them as I do
of men and women.

LEAVES OF GRASS

To think of time . . . to think through the retrospection,
  To think of today . . . and the ages continued henceforward.

Have you guessed you yourself would not continue? Have you
    dreaded those earth-beetles?
Have you feared the future would be nothing to you?

Is today nothing? Is the beginningless past nothing?
If the future is nothing they are just as surely nothing.

To think that the sun rose in the east . . . that men and women were
    flexible and real and alive . . . that every thing was real and alive;
To think that you and I did not see feel think nor bear our part,
To think that we are now here and bear our part.

Not a day passes . . . not a minute or second without an accouche-
    ment;
Not a day passes . . . not a minute or second without a corpse.

When the dull nights are over, and the dull days also,
When the soreness of lying so much in bed is over,
When the physician, after long putting off, gives the silent and terri-
    ble look for an answer,
When the children come hurried and weeping, and the brothers and
    sisters have been sent for,
When medicines stand unused on the shelf, and the camphor-smell
    has pervaded the rooms,
When the faithful hand of the living does not desert the hand of the
    dying,
When the twitching lips press lightly on the forehead of the dying,
When the breath ceases and the pulse of the heart ceases,
Then the corpse-limbs stretch on the bed, and the living look upon
    them,

They are palpable as the living are palpable.

The living look upon the corpse with their eyesight,
But without eyesight lingers a different living and looks curiously on
    the corpse.

To think that the rivers will come to flow, and the snow fall, and fruits
    ripen . . . and act upon others as upon us now . . . yet not act upon
    us;
To think of all these wonders of city and country . . . and others tak-
    ing great interest in them . . . and we taking small interest in
    them.

To think how eager we are in building our houses,
To think others shall be just as eager . . . and we quite indifferent.

I see one building the house that serves him a few years . . . or seventy
    or eighty years at most;
I see one building the house that serves him longer than that.

Slowmoving and black lines creep over the whole earth . . . they never
    cease . . . they are the burial lines,
He that was President was buried, and he that is now President shall
    surely be buried.

Cold dash of waves at the ferrywharf,
Posh and ice in the river . . . half-frozen mud in the streets,
A gray discouraged sky overhead . . . the short last daylight of
    December,
A hearse and stages . . . other vehicles give place,
The funeral of an old stagedriver . . . the cortege mostly drivers.

Rapid the trot to the cemetery,
Duly rattles the deathbell . . . the gate is passed . . . the grave is halted
    at . . . the living alight . . . the hearse uncloses,
The coffin is lowered and settled . . . the whip is laid on the coffin,
The earth is swiftly shovelled in . . . a minute . . . no one moves or
    speaks . . . it is done,
He is decently put away . . . is there anything more?

He was a goodfellow,
Freemouthed, quicktempered, not badlooking, able to take his own
    part,
Witty, sensitive to a slight, ready with life or death for a friend,
Fond of women, . . . played some . . . eat hearty and drank hearty,
Had known what it was to be flush . . . grew lowspirited toward the
    last . . . sickened . . . was helped by a contribution,

Died aged forty-one years . . . and that was his funeral.

Thumb extended or finger uplifted,
Apron, cape, gloves, strap . . . wetweather clothes . . . whip carefully
    chosen . . . boss, spotter, starter, and hostler,
Somebody loafing on you, or you loafing on somebody . . . headway
    . . . man before and man behind,
Good day's work or bad day's work . . . pet stock or mean stock . . .
    first out or last out . . . turning in at night,
To think that these are so much and so nigh to other drivers . . . and
    he there takes no interest in them.

The markets, the government, the workingman's wages . . . to think
    what account they are through our nights and days;
To think that other workingmen will make just as great account of
    them . . . yet we make little or no account.

The vulgar and the refined . . . what you call sin and what you call
    goodness . . . to think how wide a difference;
To think the difference will still continue to others, yet we lie beyond
    the difference.

To think how much pleasure there is!
Have you pleasure from looking at the sky? Have you pleasure from
    poems?
Do you enjoy yourself in the city? or engaged in business?
    or planning a nomination and election? or with your wife
    and family?
Or with your mother and sisters? or in womanly housework? or the
    beautiful maternal cares?

These also flow onward to others . . . you and I flow onward;
But in due time you and I shall take less interest in them.

Your farm and profits and crops . . . to think how engrossed you are;
To think there will still be farms and profits and crops . . . yet for you
    of what avail?

What will be will be well—for what is is well,
To take interest is well, and not to take interest shall be well.

The sky continues beautiful . . . the pleasure of men with women shall
    never be sated . . . nor the pleasure of women with men . . . nor
    the pleasure from poems;
The domestic joys, the daily housework or business, the building of
    houses—they are not phantasms . . . they have weight and form
    and location;

The farms and profits and crops . . . the markets and wages and gov-
ernment . . . they also are not phantasms;
The difference between sin and goodness is no apparition;
The earth is not an echo . . . man and his life and all the things of his
life are well-considered.

You are not thrown to the winds . . . you gather certainly and safely
around yourself,
Yourself! Yourself! Yourself forever and ever!

It is not to diffuse you that you were born of your mother and
father—it is to identify you,
It is not that you should be undecided, but that you should be
decided;
Something long preparing and formless is arrived and formed in you,
You are thenceforth secure, whatever comes or goes.

The threads that were spun are gathered . . . the weft crosses the warp
. . . the pattern is systematic.

The preparations have every one been justified;
The orchestra have tuned their instruments sufficiently . . . the baton
has given the signal.

The guest that was coming . . . he waited long for reasons . . . he is
now housed,
He is one of those who are beautiful and happy . . . he is one of those
that to look upon and be with is enough.

The law of the past cannot be eluded.
The law of the present and future cannot be eluded,
The law of the living cannot be eluded . . . it is eternal,
The law of promotion and transformation cannot be eluded,
The law of heroes and good-doers cannot be eluded,
The law of drunkards and informers and mean persons cannot be
eluded.

Slowmoving and black lines go ceaselessly over the earth,
Northerner goes carried and southerner goes carried . . . and they on
the Atlantic side and they on the Pacific, and they between, and
all through the Mississippi country . . . and all over the earth.

The great masters and kosmos are well as they go . . . the heroes and
good-doers are well,
The known leaders and inventors and the rich owners and pious and
distinguished may be well,
But there is more account than that . . . there is strict account of all.

The interminable hordes of the ignorant and wicked are not nothing,
The barbarians of Africa and Asia are not nothing,
The common people of Europe are not nothing . . . the American
    aborigines are not nothing,
A zambo or a foreheadless Crowfoot or a Camanche is not nothing,
The infected in the immigrant hospital are not nothing . . . the mur-
    derer or mean person is not nothing,
The perpetual succession of shallow people are not nothing as they
    go,
The prostitute is not nothing . . . the mocker of religion is not noth-
    ing as he goes.

I shall go with the rest . . . we have satisfaction:
I have dreamed that we are not to be changed so much . . . nor the
    law of us changed;
I have dreamed that heroes and good-doers shall be under the present
    and past law,
And that murderers and drunkards and liars shall be under the present
    and past law;
For I have dreamed that the law they are under now is enough.

And I have dreamed that the satisfaction is not so much changed . . .
    and that there is no life without satisfaction;
What is the earth? what are body and soul without satisfaction?

I shall go with the rest,
We cannot be stopped at a given point . . . that is no satisfaction;
To show us a good thing or a few good things for a space of time—
    that is no satisfaction;
We must have the indestructible breed of the best, regardless of time.

If otherwise, all these things came but to ashes of dung;
If maggots and rats ended us, then suspicion and treachery and death.

Do you suspect death? If I were to suspect death I should die now,
Do you think I could walk pleasantly and well-suited toward
    annihilation?

Pleasantly and well-suited I walk,
Whither I walk I cannot define, but I know it is good,
The whole universe indicates that it is good,
The past and the present indicate that it is good.

How beautiful and perfect are the animals! How perfect is my soul!
How perfect the earth, and the minutest thing upon it!
What is called good is perfect, and what is called sin is just as perfect;

The vegetables and minerals are all perfect . . . and the imponderable
    fluids are perfect;
Slowly and surely they have passed on to this, and slowly and surely
    they will yet pass on.

O my soul! if I realize you I have satisfaction,
Animals and vegetables! if I realize you I have satisfaction,
Laws of the earth and air! if I realize you I have satisfaction.

I cannot define my satisfaction . . . yet it is so,
I cannot define my life . . . yet it is so.

I swear I see now that every thing has an eternal soul!
The trees have, rooted in the ground . . . the weeds of the sea have . . .
    the animals.

I swear I think there is nothing but immortality!
That the exquisite scheme is for it, and the nebulous float is for it, and
    the cohering is for it,
And all preparation is for it . . . and identity is for it . . . and life and
    death are for it.

LEAVES OF GRASS

I WANDER all night in my vision,
  Stepping with light feet . . . swiftly and noiselessly stepping and
    stopping,
Bending with open eyes over the shut eyes of sleepers;
Wandering and confused . . . lost to myself . . . ill-assorted . . .
    contradictory,
Pausing and gazing and bending and stopping.

How solemn they look there, stretched and still;
How quiet they breathe, the little children in their cradles.

The wretched features of ennuyees, the white features of corpses, the
    livid faces of drunkards, the sick-gray faces of onanists,
The gashed bodies on battlefields, the insane in their strong-doored
    rooms, the sacred idiots,
The newborn emerging from gates and the dying emerging from
    gates,
The night pervades them and enfolds them.

The married couple sleep calmly in their bed, he with his palm on the
    hip of the wife, and she with her palm on the hip of the
    husband,
The sisters sleep lovingly side by side in their bed,
The men sleep lovingly side by side in theirs,
And the mother sleeps with her little child carefully wrapped.

The blind sleep, and the deaf and dumb sleep,
The prisoner sleeps well in the prison . . . the runaway son sleeps,
The murderer that is to be hung next day . . . how does he sleep?
And the murdered person . . . how does he sleep?

The female that loves unrequited sleeps,
And the male that loves unrequited sleeps;
The head of the moneymaker that plotted all day sleeps,
And the enraged and treacherous dispositions sleep.

I stand with drooping eyes by the worstsuffering and restless,
I pass my hands soothingly to and fro a few inches from them;
The restless sink in their beds . . . they fitfully sleep.

The earth recedes from me into the night,
I saw that it was beautiful . . . and I see that what is not the earth is
    beautiful.

I go from bedside to bedside . . . I sleep close with the other sleepers,
    each in turn;
I dream in my dream all the dreams of the other dreamers,
And I become the other dreamers.

I am a dance . . . Play up there! the fit is whirling me fast.

I am the everlaughing . . . it is new moon and twilight,
I see the hiding of douceurs . . . I see nimble ghosts whichever way
    I look,
Cache and cache again deep in the ground and sea, and where it is
    neither ground or sea.

Well do they do their jobs, those journeymen divine,
Only from me can they hide nothing and would not if they could;
I reckon I am their boss, and they make me a pet besides,
And surround me, and lead me and run ahead when I walk,
And lift their cunning covers and signify me with stretched arms, and
    resume the way;
Onward we move, a gay gang of blackguards with mirthshouting
    music and wildflapping pennants of joy.

I am the actor and the actress . . . the voter . . . the politician,
The emigrant and the exile . . . the criminal that stood in the box,
He who has been famous, and he who shall be famous after today,
The stammerer . . . the wellformed person . . . the wasted or feeble person.

I am she who adorned herself and folded her hair expectantly,
My truant lover has come and it is dark.

Double yourself and receive me darkness,
Receive me and my lover too . . . he will not let me go without him.

I roll myself upon you as upon a bed . . . I resign myself to the dusk.

He whom I call answers me and takes the place of my lover,
He rises with me silently from the bed.

Darkness you are gentler than my lover . . . his flesh was sweaty and
    panting,

I feel the hot moisture yet that he left me.

My hands are spread forth . . . I pass them in all directions,
I would sound up the shadowy shore to which you are journeying.

Be careful, darkness . . . already, what was it touched me?
I thought my lover had gone . . . else darkness and he are one,
I hear the heart-beat . . . I follow . . . I fade away.

O hotcheeked and blushing! O foolish hectic!
O for pity's sake, no one must see me now! . . . my clothes were stolen
     while I was abed,
Now I am thrust forth, where shall I run?

Pier that I saw dimly last night when I looked from the windows,
Pier out from the main, let me catch myself with you and stay . . .
     I will not chafe you;
I feel ashamed to go naked about the world,
And am curious to know where my feet stand . . . and what is this
     flooding me, childhood or manhood . . . and the hunger that
     crosses the bridge between.

The cloth laps a first sweet eating and drinking,
Laps life-swelling yolks . . . laps ear of rose-corn, milky and just
     ripened:
The white teeth stay, and the boss-tooth advances in darkness,
And liquor is spilled on lips and bosoms by touching glasses, and the
     best liquor afterward.

I descend my western course . . . my sinews are flaccid,
Perfume and youth course through me, and I am their wake.

It is my face yellow and wrinkled instead of the old woman's,
I sit low in a strawbottom chair and carefully darn my grandson's
     stockings.

It is I too . . . the sleepless widow looking out on the winter
     midnight,
I see the sparkles of starshine on the icy and pallid earth.

A shroud I see—and I am the shroud . . . I wrap a body and lie in the
     coffin;
It is dark here underground . . . it is not evil or pain here . . . it is blank
     here, for reasons.

It seems to me that everything in the light and air ought to be happy;
Whoever is not in his coffin and the dark grave, let him know he has
     enough.

I see a beautiful gigantic swimmer swimming naked through the
   eddies of the sea,
His brown hair lies close and even to his head . . . he strikes out with
   courageous arms . . . he urges himself with his legs.

I see his white body . . . I see his undaunted eyes;
I hate the swift-running eddies that would dash him headforemost on
   the rocks.

What are you doing you ruffianly red-trickled waves?
Will you kill the courageous giant? Will you kill him in the prime of
   his middle age?

Steady and long he struggles;
He is baffled and banged and bruised . . . he holds out while his
   strength holds out,
The slapping eddies are spotted with his blood . . . they bear him away
   . . . they roll him and swing him and turn him:
His beautiful body is borne in the circling eddies . . . it is continually
   bruised on rocks,
Swiftly and out of sight is borne the brave corpse.

I turn but do not extricate myself;
Confused . . . a pastreading . . . another, but with darkness yet.

The beach is cut by the razory ice-wind . . . the wreck-guns sound,
The tempest lulls and the moon comes floundering through the drifts.

I look where the ship helplessly heads end on . . . I hear the burst as
   she strikes . . . I hear the howls of dismay . . . they grow fainter
   and fainter.

I cannot aid with my wringing fingers;
I can but rush to the surf and let it drench me and freeze upon me.

I search with the crowd . . . not one of the company is washed to us
   alive;
In the morning I help pick up the dead and lay them in rows in a barn.

Now of the old war-days . . . the defeat at Brooklyn;
Washington stands inside the lines . . . he stands on the entrenched hills
   amid a crowd of officers,
His face is cold and damp . . . he cannot repress the weeping drops . . .
   he lifts the glass perpetually to his eyes . . . the color is blanched
   from his cheeks,
He sees the slaughter of the southern braves confided to him by their
   parents.

The same at last and at last when peace is declared,
He stands in the room of the old tavern . . . the wellbeloved soldiers
    all pass through,
The officers speechless and slow draw near in their turns,
The chief encircles their necks with his arm and kisses them on the
    cheek,
He kisses lightly the wet cheeks one after another . . . he shakes hands
    and bids goodbye to the army.

Now I tell what my mother told me today as we sat at dinner
    together,
Of when she was a nearly grown girl living home with her parents on
    the old homestead.

A red squaw came one breakfasttime to the old homestead,
On her back she carried a bundle of rushes for rushbottoming chairs;
Her hair straight shiny coarse black and profuse halfenveloped her
    face,
Her step was free and elastic . . . her voice sounded exquisitely as she
    spoke.

My mother looked in delight and amazement at the stranger,
She looked at the beauty of her tallborne face and full and pliant
    limbs,
The more she looked upon her she loved her,
Never before had she seen such wonderful beauty and purity;
She made her sit on a bench by the jamb of the fireplace . . . she
    cooked food for her,
She had no work to give her but she gave her remembrance and
    fondness.

The red squaw staid all the forenoon, and toward the middle of the
    afternoon she went away;
O my mother was loth to have her go away,
All the week she thought of her . . . she watched for her many
    a month,
She remembered her many a winter and many a summer,
But the red squaw never came nor was heard of there again.

Now Lucifer was not dead . . . or if he was I am his sorrowful terri-
    ble heir;
I have been wronged . . . I am oppressed . . . I hate him that oppresses
    me,
I will either destroy him, or he shall release me.

Damn him! how he does defile me,

How he informs against my brother and sister and takes pay for their
 blood,
How he laughs when I look down the bend after the steamboat that
 carries away my woman.

Now the vast dusk bulk that is the whale's bulk ... it seems mine,
Warily, sportsman! though I lie so sleepy and sluggish, my tap is death.

A show of the summer softness ... a contact of something unseen ...
 an amour of the light and air;
I am jealous and overwhelmed with friendliness,
And will go gallivant with the light and the air myself,
And have an unseen something to be in contact with them also.

O love and summer! you are in the dreams and in me,
Autumn and winter are in the dreams ... the farmer goes with his thrift,
The droves and crops increase ... the barns are wellfilled.

Elements merge in the night ... ships make tacks in the dreams ...
 the sailor sails ... the exile returns home,
The fugitive returns unharmed ... the immigrant is back beyond
 months and years;
The poor Irishman lives in the simple house of his childhood, with
 the wellknown neighbors and faces,
They warmly welcome him ... he is barefoot again ... he forgets he
 is welloff;
The Dutchman voyages home, and the Scotchman and Welchman
 voyage home ... and the native of the Mediterranean voyages
 home;
To every port of England and France and Spain enter wellfilled ships;
The Swiss foots it toward his hills ... the Prussian goes his way, and
 the Hungarian his way, and the Pole goes his way,
The Swede returns, and the Dane and Norwegian return.

The homeward bound and the outward bound,
The beautiful lost swimmer, the ennuyee, the onanist, the female that
 loves unrequited, the moneymaker,
The actor and actress ... those through with their parts and those
 waiting to commence,
The affectionate boy, the husband and wife, the voter, the nominee
 that is chosen and the nominee that has failed,
The great already known, and the great anytime after to day,
The stammerer, the sick, the perfectformed, the homely,
The criminal that stood in the box, the judge that sat and sentenced
 him, the fluent lawyers, the jury, the audience,

The laugher and weeper, the dancer, the midnight widow, the red
squaw,
The consumptive, the erysipalite, the idiot, he that is wronged,
The antipodes, and every one between this and them in the dark,
I swear they are averaged now . . . one is no better than the other,
The night and sleep have likened them and restored them.

I swear they are all beautiful,
Every one that sleeps is beautiful . . . every thing in the dim night is
beautiful,
The wildest and bloodiest is over and all is peace.

Peace is always beautiful,
The myth of heaven indicates peace and night.

The myth of heaven indicates the soul;
The soul is always beautiful . . . it appears more or it appears less . . .
it comes or lags behind,
It comes from its embowered garden and looks pleasantly on itself and
encloses the world;
Perfect and clean the genitals previously jetting, and perfect and clean
the womb cohering,
The head wellgrown and proportioned and plumb, and the bowels
and joints proportioned and plumb.

The soul is always beautiful,
The universe is duly in order . . . every thing is in its place,
What is arrived is in its place, and what waits is in its place;
The twisted skull waits . . . the watery or rotten blood waits,
The child of the glutton or venerealee waits long, and the child of the
drunkard waits long, and the drunkard himself waits long,
The sleepers that lived and died wait . . . the far advanced are to go on
in their turns, and the far behind are to go on in their turns,
The diverse shall be no less diverse, but they shall flow and unite . . .
they unite now.

The sleepers are very beautiful as they lie unclothed,
They flow hand in hand over the whole earth from east to west as
they lie unclothed;
The Asiatic and African are hand in hand . . . the European and
American are hand in hand,
Learned and unlearned are hand in hand . . . and male and female are
hand in hand;
The bare arm of the girl crosses the bare breast of her lover . . . they
press close without lust . . . his lips press her neck,

The father holds his grown or ungrown son in his arms with mea-
sureless love . . . and the son holds the father in his arms with
measureless love,
The white hair of the mother shines on the white wrist of the
daughter,
The breath of the boy goes with the breath of the man . . . friend is
inarmed by friend,
The scholar kisses the teacher and the teacher kisses the scholar . . .
the wronged is made right,
The call of the slave is one with the master's call . . . and the master
salutes the slave,
The felon steps forth from the prison . . . the insane becomes sane . . .
the suffering of sick persons is relieved,
The sweatings and fevers stop . . . the throat that was unsound is sound
. . . the lungs of the consumptive are resumed . . . the poor dis-
tressed head is free,
The joints of the rheumatic move as smoothly as ever, and smoother
than ever,
Stiflings and passages open . . . the paralysed become supple,
The swelled and convulsed and congested awake to themselves in
condition,
They pass the invigoration of the night and the chemistry of the night
and awake.

I too pass from the night;
I stay awhile away O night, but I return to you again and love you;
Why should I be afraid to trust myself to you?
I am not afraid . . . I have been well brought forward by you;
I love the rich running day, but I do not desert her in whom I lay so
long;
I know not how I came of you, and I know not where I go with you
. . . but I know I came well and shall go well.

I will stop only a time with the night . . . and rise betimes.

I will duly pass the day O my mother and duly return to you;
Not you will yield forth the dawn again more surely than you will
yield forth me again,
Not the womb yields the babe in its time more surely than I shall be
yielded from you in my time.

LEAVES OF GRASS

THE bodies of men and women engirth me, and I engirth them,
   They will not let me off nor I them till I go with them and
   respond to them and love them.

Was it dreamed whether those who corrupted their own live bodies
   could conceal themselves?
And whether those who defiled the living were as bad as they who
   defiled the dead?

The expression of the body of man or woman balks account,
The male is perfect and that of the female is perfect.

The expression of a wellmade man appears not only in his face,
It is in his limbs and joints also . . . it is curiously in the joints of his
   hips and wrists,
It is in his walk . . . the carriage of his neck . . . the flex of his waist
   and knees . . . dress does not hide him,
The strong sweet supple quality he has strikes through the cotton and
   flannel;
To see him pass conveys as much as the best poem . . . perhaps more,
You linger to see his back and the back of his neck and shoulderside.

The sprawl and fulness of babes . . . the bosoms and heads of women
   . . . the folds of their dress . . . their style as we pass in the street
   . . . the contour of their shape downwards;
The swimmer naked in the swimmingbath . . . seen as he swims
   through the salt transparent greenshine, or lies on his back and
   rolls silently with the heave of the water;
Framers bare-armed framing a house . . . hoisting the beams in their
   places . . . or using the mallet and mortising-chisel,
The bending forward and backward of rowers in rowboats . . . the
   horseman in his saddle;
Girls and mothers and housekeepers in all their exquisite offices,

The group of laborers seated at noontime with their open dinnerket-
tles, and their wives waiting,

The female soothing a child . . . the farmer's daughter in the garden
or cowyard,

The woodman rapidly swinging his axe in the woods . . . the young
fellow hoeing corn . . . the sleighdriver guiding his six horses
through the crowd,

The wrestle of wrestlers . . . two apprentice-boys, quite grown, lusty,
goodnatured, nativeborn, out on the vacant lot at sundown after
work,

The coats vests and caps thrown down . . . the embrace of love and
resistance,

The upperhold and underhold—the hair rumpled over and blinding
the eyes;

The march of firemen in their own costumes—the play of the mas-
culine muscle through cleansetting trowsers and waistbands,

The slow return from the fire . . . the pause when the bell strikes sud-
denly again—the listening on the alert,

The natural perfect and varied attitudes . . . the bent head, the curved
neck, the counting:

Suchlike I love . . . I loosen myself and pass freely . . . and am at the
mother's breast with the little child,

And swim with the swimmer, and wrestle with wrestlers, and march
in line with the firemen, and pause and listen and count.

I knew a man . . . he was a common farmer . . . he was the father of
five sons . . . and in them were the fathers of sons . . . and in them
were the fathers of sons.

This man was of wonderful vigor and calmness and beauty of person;

The shape of his head, the richness and breadth of his manners, the
pale yellow and white of his hair and beard, the immeasurable
meaning of his black eyes,

These I used to go and visit him to see . . . He was wise also,

He was six feet tall . . . he was over eighty years old . . . his sons were
massive clean bearded tanfaced and handsome,

They and his daughters loved him . . . all who saw him loved him . . .
they did not love him by allowance . . . they loved him with per-
sonal love;

He drank water only . . . the blood showed like scarlet through the
clear brown skin of his face;

He was a frequent gunner and fisher . . . he sailed his boat himself . . .
he had a fine one presented to him by a shipjoiner . . . he had
fowling-pieces, presented to him by men that loved him;

When he went with his five sons and many grandsons to hunt or fish
  you would pick him out as the most beautiful and vigorous of
  the gang,
You would wish long and long to be with him ... you would wish to
  sit by him in the boat that you and he might touch each other.

I have perceived that to be with those I like is enough,
To stop in company with the rest at evening is enough,
To be surrounded by beautiful curious breathing laughing flesh is
  enough,
To pass among them ... to touch any one ... to rest my arm ever so
  lightly round his or her neck for a moment ... what is this then?
I do not ask any more delight ... I swim in it as in a sea.

There is something in staying close to men and women and looking
  on them and in the contact and odor of them that pleases the
  soul well,
All things please the soul, but these please the soul well.

This is the female form,
A divine nimbus exhales from it from head to foot,
It attracts with fierce undeniable attraction,
I am drawn by its breath as if I were no more than a helpless vapor ...
  all falls aside but myself and it,
Books, art, religion, time ... the visible and solid earth ... the atmos-
  phere and the fringed clouds ... what was expected of heaven or
  feared of hell are now consumed,
Mad filaments, ungovernable shoots play out of it ... the response
  likewise ungovernable,
Hair, bosom, hips, bend of legs, negligent falling hands—all diffused
  ... mine too diffused,
Ebb stung by the flow, and flow stung by the ebb ... loveflesh swelling
  and deliciously aching,
Limitless limpid jets of love hot and enormous ... quivering jelly of
  love ... white-blow and delirious juice,
Bridegroom-night of love working surely and softly into the prostrate
  dawn,
Undulating into the willing and yielding day,
Lost in the cleave of the clasping and sweetfleshed day.

This is the nucleus ... after the child is born of woman the man is
  born of woman,
This is the bath of birth ... this is the merge of small and large and
  the outlet again.

Be not ashamed women . . . your privilege encloses the rest . . . it is
the exit of the rest,
You are the gates of the body and you are the gates of the soul.

The female contains all qualities and tempers them . . . she is in her
place . . . she moves with perfect balance,
She is all things duly veiled . . . she is both passive and active . . . she is
to conceive daughters as well as sons and sons as well as daughters.

As I see my soul reflected in nature . . . as I see through a mist one
with inexpressible completeness and beauty . . . see the bent head
and arms folded over the breast . . . the female I see,
I see the bearer of the great fruit which is immortality . . . the good
thereof is not tasted by roues, and never can be.

The male is not less the soul, nor more . . . he too is in his place,
He too is all qualities . . . he is action and power . . . the flush of the
known universe is in him,
Scorn becomes him well and appetite and defiance become him well,
The fiercest largest passions . . . bliss that is utmost and sorrow that is
utmost become him well . . . pride is for him,
The fullspread pride of man is calming and excellent to the soul;
Knowledge becomes him . . . he likes it always . . . he brings every-
thing to the test of himself,
Whatever the survey . . . whatever the sea and the sail, he strikes
soundings at last only here,
Where else does he strike soundings except here?

The man's body is sacred and the woman's body is sacred . . . it is no
matter who,
Is it a slave? Is it one of the dullfaced immigrants just landed on the
wharf?

Each belongs here or anywhere just as much as the welloff . . . just as
much as you,
Each has his or her place in the procession.

All is a procession,
The universe is a procession with measured and beautiful motion.

Do you know so much that you call the slave or the dullface ignorant?
Do you suppose you have a right to a good sight . . . and he or she has
no right to a sight?
Do you think matter has cohered together from its diffused float, and
the soil is on the surface and water runs and vegetation sprouts
for you . . . and not for him and her?

A slave at auction!
I help the auctioneer . . . the sloven does not half know his business.

Gentlemen look on this curious creature,
Whatever the bids of the bidders they cannot be high enough for
    him,
For him the globe lay preparing quintillions of years without one
    animal or plant,
For him the revolving cycles truly and steadily rolled.

In that head the allbaffling brain,
In it and below it the making of the attributes of heroes.

Examine these limbs, red black or white . . . they are very cunning in
    tendon and nerve;
They shall be stript that you may see them.

Exquisite senses, lifelit eyes, pluck, volition,
Flakes of breastmuscle, pliant backbone and neck, flesh not flabby,
    goodsized arms and legs,
And wonders within there yet.

Within there runs his blood . . . the same old blood . . . the same red
    running blood;
There swells and jets his heart . . . There all passions and desires . . . all
    reachings and aspirations:
Do you think they are not there because they are not expressed in par-
    lors and lecture-rooms?

This is not only one man . . . he is the father of those who shall be
    fathers in their turns,
In him the start of populous states and rich republics,
Of him countless immortal lives with countless embodiments and
    enjoyments.

How do you know who shall come from the offspring of his offspring
    through the centuries?
Who might you find you have come from yourself if you could trace
    back through the centuries?

A woman at auction,
She too is not only herself . . . she is the teeming mother of mothers,
She is the bearer of them that shall grow and be mates to the mothers.

Her daughters or their daughters' daughters . . . who knows who shall
    mate with them?

Who knows through the centuries what heroes may come from
    them?

In them and of them natal love . . . in them the divine mystery . . . the
    same old beautiful mystery.

Have you ever loved a woman?
Your mother . . . is she living? . . . Have you been much with her? and
    has she been much with you?
Do you not see that these are exactly the same to all in all nations and
    times all over the earth?

If life and the soul are sacred the human body is sacred;
And the glory and sweet of a man is the token of manhood untainted,
And in man or woman a clean strong firmfibred body is beautiful as
    the most beautiful face.

Have you seen the fool that corrupted his own live body? or the fool
    that corrupted her own live body?
For they do not conceal themselves, and cannot conceal themselves.

Who degrades or defiles the living human body is cursed,
Who degrades or defiles the body of the dead is not more cursed.

LEAVES OF GRASS

Sauntering the pavement or riding the country byroad here then are faces,
Faces of friendship, precision, caution, suavity, ideality,
The spiritual prescient face, the always welcome common benevolent face,
The face of the singing of music, the grand faces of natural lawyers and judges broad at the backtop,
The faces of hunters and fishers, bulged at the brows . . . the shaved blanched faces of orthodox citizens,
The pure extravagant yearning questioning artist's face,
The welcome ugly face of some beautiful soul . . . the handsome detested or despised face,
The sacred faces of infants . . . the illuminated face of the mother of many children,
The face of an amour . . . the face of veneration,
The face as of a dream . . . the face of an immobile rock,
The face withdrawn of its good and bad . . . a castrated face,
A wild hawk . . . his wings clipped by the clipper,
A stallion that yielded at last to the thongs and knife of the gelder.

Sauntering the pavement or crossing the ceaseless ferry, here then are faces;
I see them and complain not and am content with all.

Do you suppose I could be content with all if I thought them their own finale?

This now is too lamentable a face for a man;
Some abject louse asking leave to be . . . cringing for it,
Some milknosed maggot blessing what lets it wrig to its hole.

This face is a dog's snout sniffing for garbage;
Snakes nest in that mouth . . . I hear the sibilant threat.

This face is a haze more chill than the arctic sea,
Its sleepy and wobbling icebergs crunch as they go.

This is a face of bitter herbs . . . this an emetic . . . they need no label,
And more of the drugshelf . . . laudanum, caoutchouc, or hog's lard.

This face is an epilepsy advertising and doing business . . . its wordless
    tongue gives out the unearthly cry,
Its veins down the neck distend . . . its eyes roll till they show nothing
    but their whites,
Its teeth grit . . . the palms of the hands are cut by the turned-in nails,
The man falls struggling and foaming to the ground while he specu-
    lates well.

This face is bitten by vermin and worms,
And this is some murderer's knife with a halfpulled scabbard.

This face owes to the sexton his dismalest fee,
An unceasing deathbell tolls there.

Those are really men! . . . the bosses and tufts of the great round globe!

Features of my equals, would you trick me with your creased and
    cadaverous march?
Well then you cannot trick me.

I see your rounded never-erased flow,
I see neath the rims of your haggard and mean disguises.

Splay and twist as you like . . . poke with the tangling fores of fishes
    or rats,
You'll be unmuzzled . . . you certainly will.

I saw the face of the most smeared and slobbering idiot they had at
    the asylum,
And I knew for my consolation what they knew not;
I knew of the agents that emptied and broke my brother,
The same wait to clear the rubbish from the fallen tenement;
And I shall look again in a score or two of ages,
And I shall meet the real landlord perfect and unharmed, every inch
    as good as myself.

The Lord advances and yet advances:
Always the shadow in front . . . always the reached hand bringing up
    the laggards.

Out of this face emerge banners and horses . . . O superb! . . . I see
    what is coming,

I see the high pioneercaps . . . I see the staves of runners clearing the
way,
I hear victorious drums.

This face is a lifeboat;
This is the face commanding and bearded . . . it asks no odds of the
rest;
This face is flavored fruit ready for eating;
This face of a healthy honest boy is the programme of all good.

These faces bear testimony slumbering or awake,
They show their descent from the Master himself.

Off the word I have spoken I except not one . . . red white or black,
all are deific,
In each house is the ovum . . . it comes forth after a thousand years.

Spots or cracks at the windows do not disturb me,
Tall and sufficient stand behind and make signs to me;
I read the promise and patiently wait.

This is a fullgrown lily's face,
She speaks to the limber-hip'd man near the garden pickets,
Come here, she blushingly cries . . . Come nigh to me limber-hip'd
man and give me your finger and thumb,
Stand at my side till I lean as high as I can upon you,
Fill me with albescent honey . . . bend down to me,
Rub to me with your chafing beard . . . rub to my breast and
shoulders.

The old face of the mother of many children:
Whist! I am fully content.

Lulled and late is the smoke of the Sabbath morning,
It hangs low over the rows of trees by the fences,
It hangs thin by the sassafras, the wildcherry and the catbrier under
them.

I saw the rich ladies in full dress at the soiree,
I heard what the run of poets were saying so long,
Heard who sprang in crimson youth from the white froth and the
water-blue.

Behold a woman!
She looks out from her quaker cap . . . her face is clearer and more
beautiful than the sky.

She sits in an armchair under the shaded porch of the farmhouse,

The sun just shines on her old white head.

Her ample gown is of creamhued linen,
Her grandsons raised the flax, and her granddaughters spun it with the
    distaff and the wheel.

The melodious character of the earth!
The finish beyond which philosophy cannot go and does not wish to
    go!
The justified mother of men!

A YOUNG man came to me with a message from his brother,
    How should the young man know the whether and when of his
    brother?
Tell him to send me the signs.

And I stood before the young man face to face, and took his right
    hand in my left hand and his left hand in my right hand,
And I answered for his brother and for men . . . and I answered for the
    poet, and sent these signs.

Him all wait for . . . him all yield up to . . . his word is decisive and
    final,
Him they accept . . . in him lave . . . in him perceive themselves as amid
    light,
Him they immerse, and he immerses them.

Beautiful women, the haughtiest nations, laws, the landscape, people
    and animals,
The profound earth and its attributes, and the unquiet ocean,
All enjoyments and properties, and money, and whatever money will
    buy,
The best farms . . . others toiling and planting, and he unavoidably
    reaps,
The noblest and costliest cities . . . others grading and building, and he
    domiciles there;
Nothing for any one but what is for him . . . near and far are for him,
The ships in the offing . . . the perpetual shows and marches on land
    are for him if they are for any body.

He puts things in their attitudes,
He puts today out of himself with plasticity and love,
He places his own city, times, reminiscences, parents, brothers and

sisters, associations employment and politics, so that the rest
never shame them afterward, nor assume to command them.

He is the answerer,
What can be answered he answers, and what cannot be answered he
shows how it cannot be answered.

A man is a summons and challenge,
It is vain to skulk ... Do you hear that mocking and laughter? Do you
hear the ironical echoes?

Books friendships philosophers priests action pleasure pride beat up
and down seeking to give satisfaction;
He indicates the satisfaction, and indicates them that beat up and
down also.

Whichever the sex ... whatever the season or place he may go freshly
and gently and safely by day or by night,
He has the passkey of hearts ... to him the response of the prying of
hands on the knobs.

His welcome is universal ... the flow of beauty is not more welcome
or universal than he is,
The person he favors by day or sleeps with at night is blessed.

Every existence has its idiom ... every thing has an idiom and tongue;
He resolves all tongues into his own, and bestows it upon men ... and
any man translates ... and any man translates himself also:
One part does not counteract another part ... He is the joiner ...
he sees how they join.

He says indifferently and alike, How are you friend? to the President
at his levee,
And he says Good day my brother, to Cudge that hoes in the
sugarfield;
And both understand him and know that his speech is right.

He walks with perfect ease in the capitol,
He walks among the Congress ... and one representative says to
another, Here is our equal appearing and new.

Then the mechanics take him for a mechanic,
And the soldiers suppose him to be a captain ... and the sailors that
he has followed the sea,
And the authors take him for an author ... and the artists for an artist,
And the laborers perceive he could labor with them and love
them;

No matter what the work is, that he is one to follow it or has followed
    it,
No matter what the nation, that he might find his brothers and sisters
    there.

The English believe he comes of their English stock,
A Jew to the Jew he seems . . . a Russ to the Russ . . . usual and near
    . . . removed from none.

Whoever he looks at in the traveler's coffeehouse claims him,
The Italian or Frenchman is sure, and the German is sure, and the
    Spaniard is sure . . . and the island Cuban is sure.

The engineer, the deckhand on the great lakes or on the Mississippi
    or St Lawrence or Sacramento or Hudson or Delaware claims
    him.

The gentleman of perfect blood acknowledges his perfect blood,
The insulter, the prostitute, the angry person, the beggar, see them-
    selves in the ways of him . . . he strangely transmutes them,
They are not vile any more . . . they hardly know themselves, they are
    so grown.

You think it would be good to be the writer of melodious verses,
Well it would be good to be the writer of melodious verses;
But what are verses beyond the flowing character you could have? . . .
    or beyond beautiful manners and behaviour?
Or beyond one manly or affectionate deed of an apprenticeboy? . . .
    or old woman? . . . or man that has been in prison or is likely to
    be in prison?

SUDDENLY out of its stale and drowsy lair, the lair of slaves,
    Like lightning Europe le'pt forth . . . half startled at itself,
Its feet upon the ashes and the rags . . . Its hands tight to the throats of
    kings.

O hope and faith! O aching close of lives! O many a sickened heart!
Turn back unto this day, and make yourselves afresh.

And you, paid to defile the People . . . you liars mark:
Not for numberless agonies, murders, lusts,
For court thieving in its manifold mean forms,
Worming from his simplicity the poor man's wages;

For many a promise sworn by royal lips, And broken, and laughed at
 in the breaking,
Then in their power not for all these did the blows strike of personal
 revenge . . . or the heads of the nobles fall;
The People scorned the ferocity of kings.

But the sweetness of mercy brewed bitter destruction, and the fright-
 ened rulers come back:
Each comes in state with his train . . . hangman, priest and tax-
 gatherer . . . soldier, lawyer, jailer and sycophant.

Yet behind all, lo, a Shape,
Vague as the night, draped interminably, head front and form in scar-
 let folds,
Whose face and eyes none may see,
Out of its robes only this . . . the red robes, lifted by the arm,
One finger pointed high over the top, like the head of a snake appears.

Meanwhile corpses lie in new-made graves . . . bloody corpses of
 young men:
The rope of the gibbet hangs heavily . . . the bullets of princes are fly-
 ing . . . the creatures of power laugh aloud,
And all these things bear fruits . . . and they are good.

Those corpses of young men,
Those martyrs that hang from the gibbets . . . those hearts pierced by
 the gray lead,
Cold and motionless as they seem . . . live elsewhere with unslaugh-
 ter'd vitality.

They live in other young men, O kings,
They live in brothers, again ready to defy you:
They were purified by death . . . They were taught and exalted.

Not a grave of the murdered for freedom but grows seed for freedom
 . . . in its turn to bear seed,
Which the winds carry afar and re-sow, and the rains and the snows
 nourish.

Not a disembodied spirit can the weapons of tyrants let loose,
But it stalks invisibly over the earth . . . whispering counseling cautioning.

Liberty let others despair of you . . . I never despair of you.

Is the house shut? Is the master away?
Nevertheless be ready . . . be not weary of watching,
He will soon return . . . his messengers come anon.

CLEAR the way there Jonathan!
    Way for the President's marshal! Way for the government
    cannon!
Way for the federal foot and dragoons . . . and the phantoms afterward.

I rose this morning early to get betimes in Boston town;
Here's a good place at the corner . . . I must stand and see the show.

I love to look on the stars and stripes . . . I hope the fifes will play
    Yankee Doodle.

How bright shine the foremost with cutlasses,
Every man holds his revolver . . . marching stiff through Boston town.

A fog follows . . . antiques of the same come limping,
Some appear wooden-legged and some appear bandaged and
    bloodless.

Why this is a show! It has called the dead out of the earth,
The old graveyards of the hills have hurried to see;
Uncountable phantoms gather by flank and rear of it,
Cocked hats of mothy mould and crutches made of mist,
Arms in slings and old men leaning on young men's shoulders.

What troubles you, Yankee phantoms? What is all this chattering of
    bare gums?
Does the ague convulse your limbs? Do you mistake your crutches for
    firelocks, and level them?

If you blind your eyes with tears you will not see the President's
    marshal,
If you groan such groans you might balk the government cannon.

For shame old maniacs! . . . Bring down those tossed arms, and let your
    white hair be;
Here gape your smart grandsons . . . their wives gaze at them from the
    windows,
See how well-dressed . . . see how orderly they conduct themselves.

Worse and worse . . . Can't you stand it? Are you retreating?
Is this hour with the living too dead for you?

Retreat then! Pell-mell! . . . Back to the hills, old limpers!
I do not think you belong here anyhow.

But there is one thing that belongs here . . . Shall I tell you what it is,
    gentlemen of Boston?

I will whisper it to the Mayor . . . he shall send a committee to England,

They shall get a grant from the Parliament, and go with a cart to the royal vault.

Dig out King George's coffin . . . unwrap him quick from the grave-clothes . . . box up his bones for a journey:

Find a swift Yankee clipper . . . here is freight for you blackbellied clipper,

Up with your anchor! shake out your sails! . . . steer straight toward Boston bay.

Now call the President's marshal again, and bring out the government cannon,

And fetch home the roarers from Congress, and make another procession and guard it with foot and dragoons.

Here is a centrepiece for them:

Look! all orderly citizens . . . look from the windows women.

The committee open the box and set up the regal ribs and glue those that will not stay,

And clap the skull on top of the ribs, and clap a crown on top of the skull.

You have got your revenge old buster! . . . The crown is come to its own and more than its own.

Stick your hands in your pockets Jonathan . . . you are a made man from this day,

You are mighty cute . . . and here is one of your bargains.

THERE was a child went forth every day,
  And the first object he looked upon and received with wonder or pity or love or dread, that object he became,

And that object became part of him for the day or a certain part of the day . . . or for many years or stretching cycles of years.

The early lilacs became part of this child,

And grass, and white and red morningglories, and white and red clover, and the song of the phœbe-bird,

And the March-born lambs, and the sow's pink-faint litter, and the mare's foal, and the cow's calf, and the noisy brood of the barn-yard or by the mire of the pond-side . . . and the fish suspending themselves so curiously below there . . . and the beautiful curi-

ous liquid . . . and the water-plants with their graceful flat heads
 . . . all became part of him.

And the field-sprouts of April and May became part of him . . . win-
tergrain sprouts, and those of the light-yellow corn, and of the
esculent roots of the garden,
And the appletrees covered with blossoms, and the fruit afterward . . .
and woodberries . . . and the commonest weeds by the road;
And the old drunkard staggering home from the outhouse of the tav-
ern whence he had lately risen,
And the schoolmistress that passed on her way to the school . . . and
the friendly boys that passed . . . and the quarrelsome boys . . . and
the tidy and freshcheeked girls . . . and the barefoot negro boy
and girl,
And all the changes of city and country wherever he went.

His own parents . . . he that had propelled the fatherstuff at night, and
fathered him . . . and she that conceived him in her womb and
birthed him . . . they gave this child more of themselves than that,
They gave him afterward every day . . . they and of them became part
of him.

The mother at home quietly placing the dishes on the suppertable,
The mother with mild words . . . clean her cap and gown . . . a whole-
some odor falling off her person and clothes as she walks by:
The father, strong, selfsufficient, manly, mean, angered, unjust,
The blow, the quick loud word, the tight bargain, the crafty lure,
The family usages, the language, the company, the furniture . . . the
yearning and swelling heart,
Affection that will not be gainsayed . . . The sense of what is real . . .
the thought if after all it should prove unreal,
The doubts of daytime and the doubts of nighttime . . . the curious
whether and how,
Whether that which appears so is so . . . Or is it all flashes and specks?
Men and women crowding fast in the streets . . . if they are not flashes
and specks what are they?
The streets themselves, and the facades of houses . . . the goods in the
windows,
Vehicles . . . teams . . . the tiered wharves, and the huge crossing at the
ferries;
The village on the highland seen from afar at sunset . . . the river
between,
Shadows . . . aureola and mist . . . light falling on roofs and gables of
white or brown, three miles off,

The schooner near by sleepily dropping down the tide . . . the little
    boat slacktowed astern,
The hurrying tumbling waves and quickbroken crests and slapping;
The strata of colored clouds . . . the long bar of maroontint away soli-
    tary by itself . . . the spread of purity it lies motionless in,
The horizon's edge, the flying seacrow, the fragrance of saltmarsh and
    shoremud;
These became part of that child who went forth every day, and who
    now goes and will always go forth every day,
And these become of him or her that peruses them now.

WHO learns my lesson complete?
  Boss and journeyman and apprentice? . . . churchman and
  atheist?
The stupid and the wise thinker . . . parents and offspring . . . merchant
  and clerk and porter and customer . . . editor, author, artist and
  schoolboy?

Draw nigh and commence,
It is no lesson . . . it lets down the bars to a good lesson,
And that to another . . . and every one to another still.

The great laws take and effuse without argument,
I am of the same style, for I am their friend,
I love them quits and quits . . . I do not halt and make salaams.

I lie abstracted and hear beautiful tales of things and the reasons of
  things,
They are so beautiful I nudge myself to listen.

I cannot say to any person what I hear . . . I cannot say it to myself . . .
  it is very wonderful.

It is no little matter, this round and delicious globe, moving so exactly
  in its orbit forever and ever, without one jolt or the untruth of a
  single second;
I do not think it was made in six days, nor in ten thousand years, nor
  ten decillions of years,
Nor planned and built one thing after another, as an architect plans
  and builds a house.

I do not think seventy years is the time of a man or woman,
Nor that seventy millions of years is the time of a man or woman,
Nor that years will ever stop the existence of me or any one else.

Is it wonderful that I should be immortal? as every one is immortal,
I know it is wonderful . . . but my eyesight is equally wonderful . . .
  and how I was conceived in my mother's womb is equally
  wonderful,
And how I was not palpable once but am now . . . and was born on
  the last day of May 1819 . . . and passed from a babe in the creep-
  ing trance of three summers and three winters to articulate and
  walk . . . are all equally wonderful.

And that I grew six feet high . . . and that I have become a man thirty-
  six years old in 1855 . . . and that I am here anyhow—are all
  equally wonderful;

And that my soul embraces you this hour, and we affect each other
without ever seeing each other, and never perhaps to see each
other, is every bit as wonderful:
And that I can think such thoughts as these is just as wonderful,
And that I can remind you, and you think them and know them to
be true is just as wonderful,
And that the moon spins round the earth and on with the earth is
equally wonderful,
And that they balance themselves with the sun and stars is equally
wonderful.

Come I should like to hear you tell me what there is in yourself that
is not just as wonderful,
And I should like to hear the name of anything between Sunday
morning and Saturday night that is not just as wonderful.

GREAT are the myths . . . I too delight in them,
Great are Adam and Eve . . . I too look back and accept them;
Great the risen and fallen nations, and their poets, women, sages,
inventors, rulers, warriors and priests.

Great is liberty! Great is equality! I am their follower,
Helmsmen of nations, choose your craft . . . where you sail I sail,
Yours is the muscle of life or death . . . yours is the perfect science . . .
in you I have absolute faith.

Great is today, and beautiful,
It is good to live in this age . . . there never was any better.

Great are the plunges and throes and triumphs and falls of democracy,
Great the reformers with their lapses and screams,
Great the daring and venture of sailors on new explorations.

Great are yourself and myself,
We are just as good and bad as the oldest and youngest or any,
What the best and worst did we could do,
What they felt . . . do not we feel it in ourselves?
What they wished . . . do we not wish the same?

Great is youth, and equally great is old age . . . great are the day and
night;
Great is wealth and great is poverty . . . great is expression and great is
silence.

Youth large lusty and loving . . . youth full of grace and force and
fascination,
Do you know that old age may come after you with equal grace and
force and fascination?

Day fullblown and splendid . . . day of the immense sun, and action
and ambition and laughter,
The night follows close, with millions of suns, and sleep and restoring
darkness.

Wealth with the flush hand and fine clothes and hospitality:
But then the soul's wealth—which is candor and knowledge and
pride and enfolding love:
Who goes for men and women showing poverty richer than wealth?

Expression of speech . . . in what is written or said forget not that
silence is also expressive,
That anguish as hot as the hottest and contempt as cold as the coldest
may be without words,
That the true adoration is likewise without words and without
kneeling.

Great is the greatest nation . . . the nation of clusters of equal nations.

Great is the earth, and the way it became what it is,
Do you imagine it is stopped at this? . . . and the increase abandoned?
Understand then that it goes as far onward from this as this is from the
times when it lay in covering waters and gases.

Great is the quality of truth in man,
The quality of truth in man supports itself through all changes,
It is inevitably in the man . . . He and it are in love, and never leave
each other.

The truth in man is no dictum . . . it is vital as eyesight,
If there be any soul there is truth . . . if there be man or woman there
is truth . . . If there be physical or moral there is truth,
If there be equilibrium or volition there is truth . . . if there be things
at all upon the earth there is truth.

O truth of the earth! O truth of things! I am determined to press the
whole way toward you,
Sound your voice! I scale mountains or dive in the sea after you.

Great is language . . . it is the mightiest of the sciences,
It is the fulness and color and form and diversity of the earth . . . and
of men and women . . . and of all qualities and processes;

It is greater than wealth . . . it is greater than buildings or ships or religions or paintings or music.

Great is the English speech . . . What speech is so great as the English?
Great is the English brood . . . What brood has so vast a destiny as the English?
It is the mother of the brood that must rule the earth with the new rule,
The new rule shall rule as the soul rules, and as the love and justice and equality that are in the soul rule.

Great is the law . . . Great are the old few landmarks of the law . . . they are the same in all times and shall not be disturbed.

Great are marriage, commerce, newspapers, books, freetrade, railroads, steamers, international mails and telegraphs and exchanges.

Great is Justice;
Justice is not settled by legislators and laws . . . it is in the soul,
It cannot be varied by statutes any more than love or pride or the attraction of gravity can,
It is immutable . . . it does not depend on majorities . . . majorities or what not come at last before the same passionless and exact tribunal.

For justice are the grand natural lawyers and perfect judges . . . it is in their souls,
It is well assorted . . . they have not studied for nothing . . . the great includes the less,
They rule on the highest grounds . . . they oversee all eras and states and administrations.

The perfect judge fears nothing . . . he could go front to front before God,
Before the perfect judge all shall stand back . . . life and death shall stand back . . . heaven and hell shall stand back.

Great is goodness;
I do not know what it is any more than I know what health is . . . but I know it is great.

Great is wickedness . . . I find I often admire it just as much as I admire goodness:
Do you call that a paradox? It certainly is a paradox.

The eternal equilibrium of things is great, and the eternal overthrow of things is great,

And there is another paradox.

Great is life . . . and real and mystical . . . wherever and whoever,
Great is death . . . Sure as life holds all parts together, death holds all
    parts together;
Sure as the stars return again after they merge in the light, death is
    great as life.